D0029232

haruki murakami
after the quake

Born in Kyoto, Japan, in 1949, Haruki Murakami grew up in Kobe and now lives near Tokyo. The most recent of his many honors is the Yomiuri Literary Prize, whose previous recipients include Yukio Mishima, Kenzaburo Oe, and Kobo Abe. His work has been translated into twenty-seven languages.

after the quake

after the quake

stories

haruki murakami

translated from the japanese by jay rubin

Vintage International

Vintage Books

A Division of Random House, Inc.

New York

FIRST VINTAGE INTERNATIONAL EDITION,
MAY 2003

"Super-Frog Saves Tokyo" was originally published in *GQ*. "Thailand" was
originally published in *Granta*. "All God's Children Can Dance" was originally
published in *Harper's*. "UFO in Kushiro" and "Honey Pie" were originally
published in *The New Yorker*. "Landscape with Flatiron" was originally published
in *Ploughshares*.

The Library of Congress has cataloged the Knopf edition as follows:
Murakami, Haruki
[Kami no kodomo-tachi wa mina odoru. English]
After the quake: stories / Haruki Murakami; translated from the Japanese by
Jay Rubin.—1st American ed.
p. cm.
Contents: UFO in Kushiro—Landscape with flatiron—All god's children can
dance—Thailand—Super-frog saves Tokyo—Honey pie.
ISBN 0-375-41390-1 (alk. Paper)
I. Rubin, Jay, 1941– II. Title.
PL856.U673 K36 2002
895.6'35—dc21   2001038829
VINTAGE ISBN: 0-375-71327-1

"Liza! What was it yesterday, then?"

"It was what it was."

"That's impossible! That's cruel!"

—Fyodor Dostoevsky, *Demons*

r a d i o : . . . garrison already decimated by the Vietcong, who lost 115 of their men . . .

w o m a n : It's awful, isn't it, it's so anonymous.

m a n : What is?

w o m a n : They say 115 guerillas, yet it doesn't mean anything, because we don't know anything about these men, who they are, whether they love a woman, or have children, if they prefer the cinema to the theatre. We know nothing. They just say . . . 115 dead.

—Jean-Luc Godard, *Pierrot le Fou*

contents

after the quake

ufo in kushiro

Five straight days she spent in front of the television, staring at crumbled banks and hospitals, whole blocks of stores in flames, severed rail lines and expressways. She never said a word. Sunk deep in the cushions of the sofa, her mouth clamped shut, she wouldn't answer when Komura spoke to her. She wouldn't shake her head or nod. Komura could not be sure the sound of his voice was even getting through to her.

Komura's wife came from way up north in Yamagata and, as far as he knew, she had no friends or relatives who could have been hurt in Kobe. Yet she stayed rooted in front of the television from morning to night. In his presence, at least, she ate nothing and drank nothing and never went to the toilet. Aside from an occasional flick of the remote control to change the channel, she hardly moved a muscle.

Komura would make his own toast and coffee, and head off to work. When he came home in the evening, he'd fix himself a snack with whatever he found in the refrigerator and eat alone. She'd still be glaring at the late news when he dropped off to sleep. A stone wall of silence surrounded her. Komura gave up trying to break through.

When he came home from work that Sunday, the sixth day, his wife had disappeared.

Komura was a salesman at one of the oldest hi-fi-equipment specialty stores in Tokyo's Akihabara "Electronics Town." He handled top-of-the-line stuff and earned a sizeable commission whenever he made a sale. Most of his clients were doctors, wealthy independent businessmen, and rich provincials. He had been doing this for eight years and had a decent income right from the start. The economy was healthy, real-estate prices were rising, and Japan was overflowing with money. People's wallets were bursting with ten-thousand-yen bills, and everyone was dying to spend them. The most expensive items were the first to sell out.

Komura was tall and slim and a stylish dresser. He was good with people. In his bachelor days he had dated a lot of women. But after getting married, at twenty-six, he found that his desire for sexual adventures simply—and mysteriously—vanished. He hadn't slept with any woman but his wife during the five years of their marriage. Not that the opportunity had never presented itself—but he had lost all interest in fleeting affairs and one-night stands. He much preferred to come home early, have a relaxed meal with his wife, talk with her for a while on the sofa, then go to bed and make love. This was everything he wanted.

Komura's friends and colleagues were puzzled by his marriage. Alongside him with his clean, classic good looks, his wife could not have seemed more ordinary. She was short with thick arms, and she had a dull, even stolid appearance. And it wasn't just physical: there was nothing attractive about her personality either. She rarely spoke and always wore a sullen expression.

Still, though he did not quite understand why, Komura always felt his tension dissipate when he and his wife were together under one roof; it was the only time he could truly relax. He slept well with her, undisturbed by the strange dreams that had troubled him in the past. His erections were hard; his sex life was warm. He no longer had to worry about death or venereal disease or the vastness of the universe.

His wife, on the other hand, disliked Tokyo's crowds and longed for Yamagata. She missed her parents and her two elder sisters, and she would go home to see them whenever she felt the need. Her parents operated a successful inn, which kept them financially comfortable. Her father was crazy about his youngest daughter and happily paid her round-trip fares. Several times, Komura had come home from work to find his wife gone and a note on the kitchen table telling him that she was visiting her parents for a while. He never objected. He just waited for her to come back, and she always did, after a week or ten days, in a good mood.

But the letter his wife left for him when she vanished five days after the earthquake was different: *I am never coming back*, she had written, then went on to explain, simply but clearly, why she no longer wanted to live with him.

The problem is that you never give me anything, she wrote. *Or, to put it more precisely, you have nothing inside you that you can give me. You are good*

5

and kind and handsome, but living with you is like living with a chunk of air. It's not entirely your fault, though. There are lots of women who will fall in love with you. But please don't call me. Just get rid of all the stuff I'm leaving behind.

In fact, she hadn't left much of anything behind. Her clothes, her shoes, her umbrella, her coffee mug, her hair dryer: all were gone. She must have packed them in boxes and shipped them out after he left for work that morning. The only things still in the house that could be called "her stuff" were the bike she used for shopping and a few books. The Beatles and Bill Evans CDs that Komura had been collecting since his bachelor days had also vanished.

The next day, he tried calling his wife's parents in Yamagata. His mother-in-law answered the phone and told him that his wife didn't want to talk to him. She sounded somewhat apologetic. She also told him that they would be sending him the necessary forms soon and that he should put his seal on them and send them back right away.

Komura answered that he might not be able to send them "right away." This was an important matter, and he wanted time to think it over.

"You can think it over all you want, but I know it won't change anything," his mother-in-law said.

She was probably right, Komura told himself. No matter how much he thought or waited, things would never be the same. He was sure of that.

Shortly after he had sent the papers back with his seal stamped on them, Komura asked for a week's paid leave. His boss had a general idea of what had been happening, and February was a slow time of the year, so he let Komura go without a fuss. He seemed on the verge of saying something to Komura, but finally said nothing.

Sasaki, a colleague of Komura's, came over to him at lunch and said, "I hear you're taking time off. Are you planning to do something?"

"I don't know," Komura said. "What *should* I do?"

Sasaki was a bachelor, three years younger than Komura. He had a delicate build and short hair, and he wore round, gold-rimmed glasses. A lot of people thought he talked too much and had a rather arrogant air, but he got along well enough with the easygoing Komura.

"What the hell—as long as you're taking the time off, why not make a nice trip out of it?"

"Not a bad idea," Komura said.

Wiping his glasses with his handkerchief, Sasaki peered at Komura as if looking for some kind of clue.

"Have you ever been to Hokkaido?" he asked.

"Never."

"Would you like to go?"

"Why do you ask?"

Sasaki narrowed his eyes and cleared his throat. "To tell you the truth, I've got a small package I'd like to send to Kushiro, and I'm hoping you'll take it there for me. You'd be doing me a big favor, and I'd be glad to pay for a round-trip ticket. I could cover your hotel in Kushiro, too."

"A small package?"

"Like this," Sasaki said, shaping a four-inch cube with his hands. "Nothing heavy."

7

"Something to do with work?"

Sasaki shook his head. "Not at all," he said. "Strictly personal. I just don't want it to get knocked around, which is why I can't mail it. I'd like you to deliver it by hand, if possible. I really ought to do it myself, but I haven't got time to fly all the way to Hokkaido."

"Is it something important?"

His closed lips curling slightly, Sasaki nodded. "It's nothing fragile, and there are no 'hazardous materials.' There's no need to worry about it. They're not going to stop you when they X-ray it at the airport. I promise I'm not going to get you in trouble. And it weighs practically nothing. All I'm asking is that you take it along the way you'd take anything else. The only reason I'm not mailing it is I just don't *feel* like mailing it."

Hokkaido in February would be freezing cold, Komura knew, but cold or hot it was all the same to him.

"So who do I give the package to?"

"My sister. My younger sister. She lives up there."

Komura decided to accept Sasaki's offer. He hadn't thought about how to spend his week off, and making plans now would have been too much trouble. Besides, he had no reason for not wanting to go to Hokkaido. Sasaki called the airline then and there, reserving a ticket to Kushiro. The flight would leave two days later, in the afternoon.

At work the next day, Sasaki handed Komura a box like the ones used for human ashes, only smaller, wrapped in manila paper. Judging from the feel, it was made of wood. As Sasaki had said, it weighed practically nothing. Broad strips of transparent tape went all around the package over the paper. Komura held it in his hands and studied it a few seconds. He gave it a little shake but he couldn't feel or hear anything moving inside.

"My sister will pick you up at the airport. And she'll be arranging a room for you," Sasaki said. "All you have to do is stand outside the gate with the package in your hands where she can see it. Don't worry, the airport's not very big."

Komura left home with the box in his suitcase, wrapped in a thick undershirt. The plane was far more crowded than he had expected. Why were all these people going from Tokyo to Kushiro in the middle of winter? he wondered.

The morning paper was full of earthquake reports. He read it from beginning to end on the plane. The number of dead was rising. Many areas were still without water or electricity, and countless people had lost their homes. Each article reported some new tragedy, but to Komura the details seemed oddly lacking in depth. All sounds reached him as far-off, monotonous echos. The only thing he could give any serious thought to was his wife as she retreated ever farther into the distance.

Mechanically he ran his eyes over the earthquake reports, stopped now and then to think about his wife, then went back to the paper. When he grew tired of this, he closed his eyes and napped. And when he woke, he thought about his wife again. Why had she followed the TV earthquake reports with such intensity, from morning to night, without eating or sleeping? What could she have seen in them?

Two young women wearing overcoats of similar design and color approached Komura at the airport. One was fair-skinned and maybe five feet six, with short hair. The area from her nose to her full upper lip was oddly extended in a way that made Komura think of shorthaired ungulates. Her companion was more like five feet one and would have been quite pretty if her nose hadn't been so small. Her long hair fell straight to her shoulders. Her ears were exposed, and there were two moles on her right earlobe which were emphasized by the earrings she wore. Both women looked to be in their mid-twenties. They took Komura to a café in the airport.

"I'm Keiko Sasaki," the taller woman said. "My brother told me how helpful you've been to him. This is my friend Shimao."

"Nice to meet you," Komura said.

"Hi," Shimao said.

"My brother tells me your wife recently passed away," Keiko Sasaki said with a respectful expression.

Komura waited a moment before answering, "No, she didn't die."

"I just talked to my brother the day before yesterday. I'm sure he said quite clearly that you'd lost your wife."

"I did. She divorced me. But as far as I know she's alive and well."

"That's odd. I couldn't possibly have misheard something so important." She gave him an injured look. Komura put a small amount of sugar in his coffee and gave it a gentle stir before taking a sip. The liquid was thin, with no taste to speak of, more sign than substance. What the hell am I doing here? he wondered.

"Well, I guess I did mishear it. I can't imagine how else to explain the mistake," Keiko Sasaki said, apparently satisfied now. She drew in a deep breath and chewed her lower lip. "Please forgive me. I was very rude."

"Don't worry about it. Either way, she's gone."

Shimao said nothing while Komura and Keiko spoke, but she smiled and kept her eyes on Komura. She seemed to like him. He could tell from her expression and her subtle body language. A brief silence fell over the three of them.

"Anyway, let me give you the important package I brought," Komura said. He unzipped his suitcase and pulled the box out of the folds of the thick ski undershirt he had wrapped it in. The thought struck him then: I was supposed to be holding this when I got off the plane. That's how they were going to recognize me. How did they know who I was?

Keiko Sasaki stretched her hands across the table, her expressionless eyes fixed on the package. After testing its weight, she did as Komura had done and gave it a few shakes by her ear. She flashed him a smile as if to signal that everything was fine, and slipped the box into her oversize shoulder bag.

"I have to make a call," she said. "Do you mind if I excuse myself for a moment?"

"Not at all," Komura said. "Feel free."

Keiko slung the bag over her shoulder and walked off toward a distant phone booth. Komura studied the way she walked. The upper half of her body was still, while everything from the hips down made large, smooth, mechanical movements. He had the strange impression that he was witnessing some moment from the past, shoved with random suddenness into the present.

"Have you been to Hokkaido before?" Shimao asked.

Komura shook his head.

"Yeah, I know. It's a long way to come."

Komura nodded, then turned to survey his surroundings. "Funny," he said, "sitting here like this, it doesn't feel as if I've come all that far."

"Because you flew. Those planes are too damn fast. Your mind can't keep up with your body."

"You may be right."

"Did you want to make such a long trip?"

"I guess so," Komura said.

"Because your wife left?"

He nodded.

"No matter how far you travel, you can never get away from yourself," Shimao said.

Komura was staring at the sugar bowl on the table as she spoke, but then he raised his eyes to hers.

"It's true," he said. "No matter how far you travel, you can never get away from yourself. It's like your shadow. It follows you everywhere."

Shimao looked hard at Komura. "I'll bet you loved her, didn't you?"

Komura dodged the question. "You're a friend of Keiko Sasaki's?"

"Right. We do stuff together."

"What kind of stuff?"

Instead of answering him, Shimao asked, "Are you hungry?"

"I wonder," Komura said. "I feel kind of hungry and kind of not."

"Let's go and eat something warm, the three of us. It'll help you relax."

Shimao drove a small four-wheel-drive Subaru. It had to have way over a hundred thousand miles on it, judging from how battered it was. The rear bumper had a huge dent in it. Keiko Sasaki sat next to Shimao, and Komura had the cramped rear seat to himself. There was nothing particularly wrong with Shimao's driving, but the noise in back was terrible, and the suspension was nearly shot. The automatic transmission slammed into gear whenever it downshifted, and the heater blew hot and cold. Shutting his eyes, Komura felt as if he had been imprisoned in a washing machine.

No snow had been allowed to gather on the streets in Kushiro, but dirty, icy mounds stood at random intervals on both sides of the road. Dense clouds hung low and, although it was not yet sunset, everything was dark and desolate. The wind tore through the city in sharp squeals. There were no pedestrians. Even the traffic lights looked frozen.

"This is one part of Hokkaido that doesn't get much snow," Keiko Sasaki explained in a loud voice, glancing back at Komura. "We're on the coast and the wind is strong, so whatever piles up gets blown away. It's cold, though, *freezing* cold. Sometimes it feels like it's taking your ears off."

"You hear about drunks who freeze to death sleeping on the street," Shimao said.

"Do you get bears around here?" Komura asked.

Keiko giggled and turned to Shimao. "Bears, he says."

Shimao gave the same kind of giggle.

"I don't know much about Hokkaido," Komura said by way of explanation.

"I know a good story about bears," Keiko said. "Right, Shimao?"

"A *great* story!" Shimao said.

But their talk broke off at that point, and neither of them told the bear story. Komura didn't ask to hear it. Soon they reached their destination, a big noodle shop on the highway. They parked in the lot and went inside. Komura had a beer and a hot bowl of ramen noodles. The place was dirty and empty, and the chairs and tables were rickety, but the ramen was excellent, and when he had finished eating, Komura did, in fact, feel a little more relaxed.

"Tell me, Mr. Komura," Keiko Sasaki said, "do you have something you want to do in Hokkaido? My brother tells me you're going to spend a week here."

Komura thought about it for a moment, but couldn't come up with anything he wanted to do.

"How about a hot spring? Would you like a nice, long soak in a tub? I know a little country place not far from here."

"Not a bad idea," Komura said.

"I'm sure you'd like it. It's really nice. No bears or anything."

The two women looked at each other and laughed again.

"Do you mind if I ask you about your wife?" Keiko said.

"I don't mind."

"When did she leave?"

"Hmm . . . five days after the earthquake, so that's more than two weeks ago now."

"Did it have something to do with the earthquake?"

Komura shook his head. "Probably not. I don't think so."

"Still, I wonder if things like that aren't connected some-how," Shimao said with a tilt of the head.

"Yeah," Keiko said. "It's just that you can't see how."

"Right," Shimao said. "Stuff like that happens all the time."

"Stuff like what?" Komura asked.

"Like, say, what happened with somebody I know," Keiko said.

"You mean Mr. Saeki?" Shimao asked.

"Exactly," Keiko said. "There's this guy—Saeki. He lives in Kushiro. He's about forty. A hairstylist. His wife saw a UFO last year, in the autumn. She was driving on the edge of town all by herself in the middle of the night and she saw a huge UFO land in a field. *Whoosh!* Like in *Close Encounters.* A week later, she left home. They weren't having any domestic prob-lems or anything. She just disappeared and never came back."

"Into thin air," Shimao said.

"And it was because of the UFO?" Komura asked.

"I don't know why," Keiko said. "She just walked out. No note or anything. She had two kids in elementary school, too. The whole week before she left, all she'd do was tell people about the UFO. You couldn't get her to stop. She'd go on and on about how big and beautiful it was."

She paused to let the story sink in.

"My wife left a note," Komura said. "And we don't have any kids."

"So your situation's a little better than Saeki's," Keiko said.

"Yeah. Kids make a big difference," Shimao said, nodding.

"Shimao's father left home when she was seven," Keiko explained with a frown. "Ran off with his wife's younger sister."

"All of a sudden. One day," Shimao said, smiling.

A silence settled over the group.

"Maybe Mr. Saeki's wife didn't run away but was captured by aliens from the UFO," Komura said to smooth things over.

"It's possible," Shimao said with a somber expression. "You hear stories like that all the time."

"You mean like you're-walking-along-the-street-and-a-bear-eats-you kind of thing?" Keiko asked. The two women laughed again.

The three of them left the noodle shop and went to a nearby love hotel. It was on the edge of town, on a street where love hotels alternated with gravestone dealers. The hotel Shimao had chosen was an odd building, constructed to look like a European castle. A triangular red flag flew on its highest tower.

Keiko got the key at the front desk, and the three of them took the elevator to the room. The windows were tiny, compared with the absurdly big bed. Komura hung his down jacket on a hanger and went into the toilet. During the few minutes he was in there, the two women managed to run a bath, dim the lights, check the heat, turn on the television, examine the delivery menus from local restaurants, test the light switches at the head of the bed, and check the contents of the minibar.

"The owners are friends of mine," Keiko said. "I had them get their biggest room ready. It *is* a love hotel, but don't let that bother you. You're not bothered, are you?"

"Not at all," Komura said.

"I thought this would make a lot more sense than sticking you in a cramped little room in some cheap business hotel by the station."

"You may be right," Komura said.

"Why don't you take a bath? I filled the tub."

Komura did as he was told. The tub was huge. He felt uneasy soaking in it alone. The couples who came to this hotel probably took baths together.

When he emerged from the bathroom, Komura was surprised to find that Keiko Sasaki had left. Shimao was still there, drinking beer and watching TV.

"Keiko went home," Shimao said. "She wanted me to apologize and tell you that she'll be back tomorrow morning. Do you mind if I stay here a little while and have a beer?"

"Fine," Komura said.

"You're sure it's no problem? Like, you want to be alone or you can't relax if somebody else is around or something?"

Komura insisted it was no problem. Drinking a beer and drying his hair with a towel, he watched TV with Shimao. It was a news special on the Kobe earthquake. The usual images appeared again and again: tilted buildings, buckled streets, old women weeping, confusion and aimless anger. When a commercial came on, Shimao used the remote to switch off the TV.

"Let's talk," she said, "as long as we're here."

"Fine," Komura said.

"Hmm, what should we talk about?"

"In the car, you and Keiko said something about a bear, remember? You said it was a great story."

"Oh yeah," she said, nodding. "The bear story."

"You want to tell it to me?"

"Sure, why not?"

Shimao got a fresh beer from the minibar and filled both their glasses.

"It's a little raunchy," she said. "You don't mind?"

Komura shook his head.

"I mean, some men don't like hearing a woman tell certain kinds of stories."

"I'm not like that."

"It's something that actually happened to me, so it's a little embarrassing."

"I'd like to hear it if you're OK with it."

"I'm OK, if you're OK."

"I'm OK," Komura said.

"Three years ago—back around the time I entered junior college—I was dating this guy. He was a year older than me, a college student. He was the first guy I had sex with. One day the two of us were out hiking—in the mountains way up north."

She took a sip of beer.

"It was fall, and the hills were full of bears. That's the time of year when the bears are getting ready to hibernate, so they're out looking for food and they're really dangerous. Sometimes they attack people. They did an awful job on one hiker just three days before we went out. So somebody gave us a bell to carry—about the same size as a wind-bell. You're supposed to shake it when you walk so the bears know there are people around and won't come out. Bears don't attack people on purpose. I mean, they're pretty much vegetarians. They don't *have* to attack people. What happens is they suddenly bump into people in their territory and they get surprised or angry and they attack out of reflex. So if you walk along ringing your bell, they'll avoid you. Get it?"

"I get it."

"So that's what we were doing, walking along and ringing the bell. We got to this place where there was nobody else around, and all of a sudden he said he wanted to . . . do it. I kind of liked the idea, too, so I said OK and we went into this bushy place off the trail where nobody could see us, and we spread out a piece of plastic. But I was afraid of the bears. I mean, think how awful it would be to have some bear attack you from behind and kill you when you're having sex! I would never want to die that way. Would you?"

Komura agreed that he would not want to die that way.

"So there we were, shaking the bell with one hand and having sex. Kept it up from start to finish. *Ding-a-ling! Ding-a-ling!*"

"Which one of you shook the bell?"

"We took turns. We'd trade off when our hands got tired. It was so weird, shaking this bell the whole time we were doing it! I think about it sometimes even now, when I'm having sex, and I start laughing."

Komura gave a little laugh, too.

Shimao clapped her hands. "Oh, that's wonderful," she said. "You *can* laugh after all!"

"Of course I can laugh," Komura said, but come to think of it, this was the first time he had laughed in quite a while. When was the last time?

"Do you mind if I take a bath, too?" Shimao asked.

"Fine," he said.

While she was bathing, Komura watched a variety show emceed by some comedian with a loud voice. He didn't find it the least bit funny, but he couldn't tell whether that was the show's fault or his own. He drank a beer and opened a pack of nuts from the minibar. Shimao stayed in the bath for a very long time. Finally, she came out wearing nothing but a towel and sat on the edge of the bed. Dropping the towel, she slid in between the sheets like a cat and lay there looking straight at Komura.

"When was the last time you did it with your wife?" she asked.

"At the end of December, I think."

"And nothing since?"

"Nothing."

"Not with anybody?"

Komura closed his eyes and shook his head.

"You know what *I* think," Shimao said. "You need to lighten up and learn to enjoy life a little more. I mean, think about it: tomorrow there could be an earthquake; you could be kidnapped by aliens; you could be eaten by a bear. Nobody knows what's going to happen."

"Nobody knows what's going to happen," Komura echoed.

"*Ding-a-ling*," Shimao said.

After several failed attempts to have sex with Shimao, Komura gave up. This had never happened to him before.

"You must have been thinking about your wife," Shimao said.

"Yup," Komura said, but in fact what he had been thinking about was the earthquake. Images of it had come to him one after another, as if in a slide show, flashing on the screen and fading away. Highways, flames, smoke, piles of rubble, cracks in streets. He couldn't break the chain of silent images.

Shimao pressed her ear against his naked chest.

"These things happen," she said.

"Uh-huh."

"You shouldn't let it bother you."

"I'll try not to," Komura said.

"Men always let it bother them, though."

Komura said nothing.

Shimao played with his nipple.

"You said your wife left a note, didn't you?"

"I did."

"What did it say?"

"That living with me was like living with a chunk of air."

"A chunk of air?" Shimao tilted her head back to look up at Komura. "What does *that* mean?"

"That there's nothing inside me, I guess."

"Is it true?"

"Could be," Komura said. "I'm not sure, though. I may have nothing inside me, but what would *something* be?"

"Yeah, really, come to think of it. What *would* something be? My mother was crazy about salmon skin. She always used to wish there were a kind of salmon made of nothing but skin. So there may be some cases when it's *better* to have nothing inside. Don't you think?"

Komura tried to imagine what a salmon made of nothing but skin would be like. But even supposing there were such a thing, wouldn't the skin itself be the *something* inside? Komura took a deep breath, raising and then lowering Shimao's head on his chest.

"I'll tell you this, though," Shimao said, "I don't know

2 1

whether you've got nothing or something inside you, but I think you're terrific. I'll bet the world is full of women who would understand you and fall in love with you."

"It said that, too."

"What? Your wife's note?"

"Uh-huh."

"No kidding," Shimao said, lowering her head to Komura's chest again. He felt her earring against his skin like a secret object.

"Come to think of it," Komura said, "what's the *something* inside that box I brought up here?"

"Is it bothering you?"

"It wasn't bothering me before. But now, I don't know, it's starting to."

"Since when?"

"Just now."

"All of a sudden?"

"Yeah, once I started thinking about it, all of a sudden."

"I wonder why it's started to bother you now, all of a sudden?"

Komura glared at the ceiling for a minute to think. "I wonder."

They listened to the moaning of the wind. The wind: it came from someplace unknown to Komura, and it blew past to someplace unknown to him.

"I'll tell you why," Shimao said in a low voice. "It's because that box contains the *something* that was inside you. You didn't know that when you carried it here and gave it to Keiko with your own hands. Now, you'll never get it back."

Komura lifted himself from the mattress and looked down at the woman. Tiny nose, moles on the earlobe. In the room's deep silence, his heart beat with a loud, dry sound. His bones cracked as he leaned forward. For one split second, Komura realized that he was on the verge of committing an act of overwhelming violence.

"Just kidding," Shimao said when she saw the look on his face. "I said the first thing that popped into my head. It was a lousy joke. I'm sorry. Try not to let it bother you. I didn't mean to hurt you."

Komura forced himself to calm down and, after a glance around the room, sank his head into his pillow again. He closed his eyes and took a deep breath. The huge bed stretched out around him like a nocturnal sea. He heard the freezing wind. The fierce pounding of his heart shook his bones.

"Are you starting to feel a *little* as if you've come a long way?" Shimao asked.

"Hmm. Now I feel as if I've come a *very* long way," Komura answered honestly.

Shimao traced a complicated design on Komura's chest with her fingertip, as if casting a magic spell.

"But really," she said, "you're just at the beginning."

landscape with flatiron

Junko was watching television when the phone rang a few minutes before midnight. Keisuke sat in the corner of the room wearing headphones, eyes half closed, head swinging back and forth as his long fingers flew over the strings of his electric guitar. He was practicing a fast passage and obviously had no idea the phone was ringing. Junko picked up the receiver.

"Did I wake you?" Miyake asked in his familiar muffled Osaka accent.

"Nah," Junko said. "We're still up."

"I'm at the beach. You should *see* all this driftwood! We can make a big one this time. Can you come down?"

"Sure," Junko said. "Let me change clothes. I'll be there in ten minutes."

She slipped on a pair of tights and then her jeans. On top she wore a turtleneck sweater, and she stuffed a pack of cigarettes into the pocket of her woolen coat. Purse, matches, key ring. She nudged Keisuke in the back with her foot. He tore off his headphones.

"I'm going for a bonfire on the beach," she said.

"Miyake again?" Keisuke asked with a scowl. "You gotta be kidding. It's February, ya know. Twelve o'clock at night! You're gonna go make a bonfire *now*?"

"That's OK, *you* don't have to come. I'll go by myself."

Keisuke sighed. "Nah, I'll come. Gimme a minute to change."

He turned off his amp, and over his pajamas he put on pants, a sweater, and a down jacket which he zipped up to his chin. Junko wrapped a scarf around her neck and put on a knitted hat.

"You guys're crazy," Keisuke said as they took the path down to the beach. "What's so great about bonfires?"

The night was cold, but there was no wind at all. Words left their mouths to hang frozen in midair.

"What's so great about Pearl Jam?" Junko said. "Just a lot of noise."

"Pearl Jam has ten million fans all over the world," Keisuke said.

"Well, bonfires have had fans all over the world for fifty thousand years," Junko said.

"You've got something there," Keisuke said.

"People will be lighting fires long after Pearl Jam is gone."

"You've got something there, too." Keisuke pulled his right hand out of his pocket and put his arm around Junko's shoulders. "The trouble is, I don't have a damn thing to do with anything fifty thousand years ago—or fifty thousand years from now, either. Nothing. Zip. What's important is *now*. Who knows when the world is gonna end? Who can think about the future? The only thing that matters is whether I can get my stomach full *right now* and get it up *right now*. Right?"

They climbed the steps to the top of the breakwater. Miyake was down in his usual spot on the beach, collecting driftwood of all shapes and sizes and making a neat pile. One huge log must have taken a major effort to drag to the spot.

The light of the moon transformed the shoreline into a sharpened sword blade. The winter waves were strangely hushed as they washed over the sand. Miyake was the only one on the beach.

"Pretty good, huh?" he said with a puff of white breath.

"Incredible!" Junko said.

"This happens every once in a while. You know, we had that stormy day with the big waves. Lately, I can tell from the sound, like, 'Today some great firewood's going to wash up.' "

"OK, OK, we know how good you are," Keisuke said, rubbing his hands together. "Now let's get warm. It's so damn cold, it's enough to shrivel your balls."

"Hey, take it easy. There's a *right* way to do this. First you've got to *plan* it. And when you've got it all arranged so it'll work without a hitch, you light it slow-like. You can't rush it. 'The patient beggar earns his keep.' "

"Yeah," Keisuke said. "Like the patient hooker earns her keep."

Miyake shook his head. "You're too young to be making such crummy jokes all the time," he said.

Miyake had done a skillful job of interlacing the bigger logs and smaller scraps until his pile had come to resemble some kind of avant-garde sculpture. Stepping back a few paces, he would examine in detail the form he had constructed, adjust some of the pieces, then circle around to the other side for

another look, repeating the process several times. As always. All
he had to do was look at the way the pieces of wood were com-
bined to begin having mental images of the subtlest movement
of the rising flames, the way a sculptor can imagine the pose of
a figure hidden in a lump of stone.

Miyake took his time, but once he had everything arranged
to his satisfaction, he nodded as if to say to himself, That's it:
perfect. Next, he bunched up sheets of newspaper that he had
brought along, slipped them through the gaps at the bottom of
the pile, and lit them with a plastic cigarette lighter. Junko took
her cigarettes from her pocket, put one in her mouth, and
struck a match. Narrowing her eyes, she stared at Miyake's
hunched back and balding head. This was it: the one heart-
stopping moment of the whole procedure. Would the fire
catch? Would it erupt in giant flames?

The three stared in silence at the mountain of driftwood.
The sheets of newspaper flared up, rose swaying in flames for a
moment, then shriveled and went out. After that there was
nothing. It didn't work, thought Junko. The wood must have
been wetter than it looked.

She was on the verge of losing hope when a plume of white
smoke shot up from the pile. With no wind to disperse it, the
smoke became an unbroken thread rising straight toward the
sky. The pile must have caught fire somewhere, but still there
was no sign of flames.

No one said a word. Even the talkative Keisuke kept his
mouth shut tight, hands shoved in coat pockets. Miyake hun-
kered down on the sand. Junko folded her arms across her

chest, cigarette in hand. She would puff on it occasionally, as if suddenly recalling that it was there.

As usual, Junko thought about Jack London's "To Build a Fire." It was the story of a man traveling alone through the snowy Alaskan interior and his attempts to light a fire. He would freeze to death unless he could make it catch. The sun was going down. Junko hadn't read much fiction, but that one short story she had read again and again, ever since her teacher had assigned it as an essay topic during the summer vacation of her first year in high school. The scene of the story would always come vividly to mind as she read. She could feel the man's fear and hope and despair as if they were her own; she could sense the very pounding of his heart as he hovered on the brink of death. Most important of all, though, was the fact that the man was fundamentally longing for death. She knew that for sure. She couldn't explain how she knew, but she knew it from the start. Death was really what he wanted. He *knew* that it was the right ending for him. And yet he had to go on fighting with all his might. He had to fight against an overwhelming adversary in order to survive. What most shook Junko was this deep-rooted contradiction.

The teacher ridiculed her view. "Death is really what he wanted? That's a new one for me! And strange! Quite 'original,' I'd have to say." He read her conclusion aloud before the class, and everybody laughed.

But Junko knew. All of them were wrong. Otherwise, how could the ending of the story be so quiet and beautiful?

"Uh, Mr. Miyake," Keisuke ventured, "don't you think the fire has gone out?"

"Don't worry, it's caught. It's just getting ready to flare up. See how it's smoking? You know what they say: 'Where there's smoke, there's fire.' "

"Well, you know what else they say: 'Where there's blood, there's a hard-on.' "

"Is that all you ever talk about?"

"No, but how can you be so sure it hasn't gone out?"

"I just know. It's going to flare up."

"How did you come to master such an art, Mr. Miyake?"

"I wouldn't call it an 'art.' I learned it when I was a Boy Scout. When you're a Scout, like it or not, you learn everything there is to know about building a fire."

"I see," said Keisuke. "A Boy Scout, huh?"

"That's not the whole story, of course. I have a kind of talent, too. I don't mean to brag, but when it comes to making a bonfire I have a special talent that most folks just don't have."

"It must give you a lot of pleasure, but I don't suppose this talent of yours makes you lots of money."

"True. None at all," Miyake said with a smile.

As he had predicted, a few small flames began to flicker at the center of the pile, accompanied by a faint crackling sound. Junko let out a long-held breath. Now there was nothing to worry about. They would have their bonfire. Facing the new-born flames, the three began to stretch out their hands. For the next few minutes there was nothing more to be done but to watch in silence as, little by little, the flames gained in strength. Those people of fifty thousand years ago must have felt like this when they held their hands out to the flames, thought Junko.

"I understand you're from Kobe, Mr. Miyake," Keisuke said in a cheery voice as if the thought had suddenly popped into his head. "Did you have relatives or something in the Kansai earthquake last month?"

"I'm not sure," said Miyake. "I don't have any ties with Kobe anymore. Not for years."

"Years? Well, you sure haven't lost your Kansai accent."

"No? I can't tell, myself."

"I do declare, you must be joking," said Keisuke in exaggerated Kansai tones.

"Cut the shit, Keisuke. The last thing I want to hear is some Ibaragi asshole trying to talk to me in a phony Kansai accent. You eastern farm boys'd be better off tearing around on your motorcycles during the slack season."

"Whoa, I sure rubbed *you* the wrong way! You *look* like a nice quiet guy, but you've got one hell of a mouth. And this place is Ibaraki, not 'Ibaragi.' All you Kansai types are ready to put us eastern 'farm boys' down at the drop of a hat. I give up," Keisuke said. "But seriously, though, did anybody get hurt? You must have had *somebody* you know in Kobe. Have you seen the news on TV?"

"Let's change the subject," Miyake said. "Whiskey?"

"You bet."

"Jun?"

"Just a little," Junko said.

Miyake pulled a thin metal flask from the pocket of his leather jacket and handed it to Keisuke, who twisted off the cap and poured some whiskey into his mouth without touching his lips to the rim. He glugged it down and sucked in a sharp breath.

"That is *great!*" he said. "This has *got* to be a twenty-one-year-old single malt! Super stuff! Aged in oak. You can hear the roar of the sea and the breath of Scottish angels."

"Give me a break, Keisuke. It's the cheapest Suntory you can buy."

Next it was Junko's turn. She took the flask from Keisuke, poured a little into the cap, and tried a few tiny sips. She grimaced, but chased after that special warm feeling as the liquid moved down from her throat to her stomach. The core of her body grew a touch warmer. Next, Miyake took one quiet swallow, and Keisuke followed him with another gulp. As the flask moved from hand to hand, the bonfire grew in size and strength—not all at once, but in slow, gradual stages. That was the great thing about Miyake's bonfires. The spread of the flames was soft and gentle, like an expert caress, with nothing rough or hurried about it—their only purpose was to warm people's hearts.

Junko never said much in the presence of the fire. She hardly moved. The flames accepted all things in silence, drank them in, understood, and forgave. A family, a *real* family, was probably like this, she thought.

Junko came to this town in May of her third year in high school. With her father's seal and passbook, she had taken three hundred thousand yen from the bank, stuffed all the clothes she could into a Boston bag, and run away from home. She transferred from one train to the next at random until she had come all the way from Tokorozawa to this little seaside spot in Ibaraki Prefecture, a town she had never even heard of. At the realtor's across from the station she found a one-room apartment, and the following week took a job at a convenience store on the coast highway. To her mother she wrote: *Don't worry about me, and please don't look for me, I'm doing fine.*

She was sick to death of school and couldn't stand the sight of her father. She had gotten on well with him when she was little. On weekends and holidays the two of them had gone everywhere together. She felt proud and strong to walk down the street holding his hand. But when her periods started near the end of elementary school, and her pubic hair began to grow, and her chest began to swell, he started to look at her in a strange new way. After she passed five-foot-six in the third year of junior high, he hardly spoke to her at all.

Plus, her grades were nothing to boast about. Near the top of her class when she entered middle school, by graduation time it would have been easier to count her place from the bottom, and she barely made it into high school. Which is not to say that she was stupid: she just couldn't concentrate. She could never finish anything she started. Whenever she tried to concentrate, her head would ache deep inside. It hurt her to breathe, and the rhythm of her heart became irregular. Attending school was absolute torture.

Not long after she settled in this new town, she met Keisuke. He was two years older, and a great surfer. He was tall, dyed his hair brown, and had beautiful straight teeth. He had settled in Ibaraki for its good surf, and formed a rock band with some friends. He was registered at a second-rate private college, but hardly ever went to campus and had zero prospects of graduating. His parents ran an old respected sweetshop in the city of Mito, and he could have carried on the family business as a last resort, but he had no intention of settling down as a sweetshop owner. All he wanted was to ride around with his friends in his Datsun truck, surf, and play the guitar in their amateur band—an easygoing lifestyle that anyone could see was not going to last forever.

Junko got friendly with Miyake after she moved in with Keisuke. Miyake seemed to be in his mid-forties—a small, slim guy with glasses, a long narrow face, and short hair. He was clean-shaven, but he had such a heavy beard that by sundown each day his face was covered in shadows. He liked to wear a faded dungaree shirt or aloha shirt, which he never tucked into his baggy old chinos, and on his feet he wore white, worn-out sneakers. In winter, he would put on a creased leather jacket and sometimes a baseball cap. Junko had never seen him in any other kind of outfit. Everything he wore, though, was spotlessly clean.

Speakers of the Kansai dialect were all but nonexistent in this place, so people noticed Miyake. "He lives alone in a rented house near here," one of the girls at work told Junko. "He paints pictures. I don't think he's famous or anything, and I've never seen his stuff. But he lives OK. He seems to manage. He goes to Tokyo sometimes and comes back late in the day with painting supplies or something. Gee, I don't know, he's maybe been here five years or so. You see him on the beach all the time making bonfires. I guess he likes them. I mean, he always has this intense look in his eyes when he's making one. He doesn't talk much, and he's kind of weird, but he's not a bad guy."

Miyake would come to the convenience store at least three times a day. In the morning he'd buy milk, bread, and a newspaper. At noon, he'd buy a box lunch, and in the evening he'd buy a cold can of beer and a snack—the same thing, day after day. He and Junko never exchanged more than the barest civilities, but she found herself drawn to him after a while.

When they were alone in the store one morning, she took a chance and asked him about himself. Why did he come in so often, even if he did live close by? Why didn't he just buy lots of milk and beer and keep it in the refrigerator? Wouldn't that be more convenient? Of course, it was all the same to the store people, but still . . .

"Yeah, I guess you're right," he said. "It'd make more sense to stock up, but I can't."

"Why not?" Junko asked.

"Well, it's just, like—I can't, that's all."

"I didn't mean to pry or anything," Junko said. "Please don't let it bother you. It's just the way I am. I can't help asking questions when I don't know something. I don't mean any harm by it."

Miyake hesitated a moment, scratching his head. Then, with some difficulty, he said, "Tell you the truth, I don't have a refrigerator. I don't *like* refrigerators."

Junko smiled. "I don't *like* refrigerators myself, but I do *have* one. Isn't it kind of inconvenient not having one?"

"Sure it's inconvenient, but I hate the things, so what can I do? I can't sleep at night when there's a refrigerator around."

What a weird guy, thought Junko. But now she was more interested in him than ever.

Walking on the beach one evening a few days later, Junko saw Miyake tending a bonfire, alone. It was a small fire made of driftwood he had collected. Junko spoke to Miyake, then joined him at the fire. Standing beside him, she was a good couple of inches taller. The two of them traded simple greetings, then said nothing at all as they stared at the fire.

It was the first time that Junko felt a certain "something" as she watched the flames of a bonfire: "something" deep down, a "wad" of feeling, she might have called it, because it was too raw, too heavy, too real to be called an idea. It coursed through her body and vanished, leaving behind a sweet-sad, chest-gripping, strange sort of feeling. For a time after it had gone, she had gooseflesh on her arms.

"Tell me, Mr. Miyake, when you see the shapes that a bonfire makes, do you ever feel kind of strange?"

"How so?"

"I don't know, it's like all of a sudden you get very clear about something people don't usually notice in everyday life. I don't know how to put it, I'm not smart enough, but watching the fire now, I get this deep, quiet kind of feeling."

Miyake thought about it a while. "You know, Jun," he said, "a fire can be any shape it wants to be. It's free. So it can look like anything at all depending on what's inside the person looking at it. If you get this deep, quiet kind of feeling when you look at a fire, that's because it's showing you the deep, quiet kind of feeling you have inside yourself. You know what I mean?"

"Uh-huh."

"But it doesn't happen with just *any* fire. For something like this to happen, the fire itself has to be free. It won't happen with a gas stove or a cigarette lighter. It won't even happen with an ordinary bonfire. For the fire to be free, you've got to make it in the right kind of place. Which isn't easy. Not just anybody can do it."

"But *you* can do it, Mr. Miyake?"

"Sometimes I can, sometimes I can't. Most of the time, I can. If I really put my mind to it, I pretty much can."

"You like bonfires, don't you?"

Miyake nodded. "It's almost a sickness with me. Why do you think I came to live in this navel-lint nothing of a town? It's because this place gets more driftwood than any other beach I know. That's the only reason. I came all the way out here to make bonfires. Kind of pointless, huh?"

Whenever she had the chance after that, Junko would join Miyake for his bonfires. He made them all year long except for midsummer, when the beach was full of people far into the night. Sometimes he would make two a week, and sometimes he would go a month without one. His pace was determined by the amount of driftwood that washed ashore. And when the time came for a fire, he would be sure to call Junko. Keisuke had an ugly jealous streak, but Miyake was the one exception. He would rib Junko about her "bonfire buddy."

The flames finally found their way to the biggest log, and now at last the bonfire was settling in for a long burn. Junko lowered herself to the sandy beach and stared at the flames with her mouth shut tight. Miyake adjusted the progress of the fire with great care, using a long branch to keep the flames from either spreading too quickly or losing strength. From his small pile of spare fuel, he would occasionally pick a length of driftwood and toss it in where it was needed.

Keisuke announced that he had a stomachache: "Must've caught a chill. Think I just need a crap."

"Why don't you go home and rest?" Junko said.

"Yeah, I really should," Keisuke said, looking sorry for himself. "How about you?"

"Don't worry about Jun," Miyake said. "I'll see her home. She'll be fine."

"OK, then. Thanks." Keisuke left the beach.

"He's such an idiot," Junko said, shaking her head. "He gets carried away and drinks too much."

"I know what you mean, Jun, but it's no good being *too* sensible when you're young. It just spoils the fun. Keisuke's got his good points, too."

"Maybe so, but he doesn't use his brain for anything."

"Some things your brain can't help you with. It's not easy being young."

The two fell silent for a while in the presence of the fire, each lost in private thoughts and letting time flow along separate paths.

Then Junko said, "You know, Mr. Miyake, something's been kind of bothering me. Do you mind if I ask you about it?"

"What kind of something?"

"Something personal."

Miyake scratched his stubbly cheeks with the flat of his hand. "Well, I don't know. I guess it'd be OK."

"I was just wondering if, maybe, you had a wife somewhere."

Miyake pulled the flask from the pocket of his leather jacket, opened it, and took a long, slow drink. Then he put on the cap, slipped the flask into his pocket, and looked at Junko.

"Where did *that* come from all of a sudden?"

"It's not all of a sudden. I kind of got the feeling before, when Keisuke started talking about the earthquake. I saw the look on your face. And you know what you once told me, about how people's eyes have something honest about them when they're watching a fire."

"I did?"

"And do you have kids, too?"

"Yup. Two of 'em."

"In Kobe, right?"

"That's where the house is. I suppose they're still living there."

"Where in Kobe?"

"The Higashi-Nada section. Up in the hills. Not much damage there."

Miyake narrowed his eyes, raised his face, and looked out at the dark sea. Then he turned his eyes back to the fire.

"That's why I can't blame Keisuke," he said. "I can't call him an idiot. I don't have the right. I'm not using my brain any more than he is. I'm the idiot king. I think you know what I mean."

"Do you want to tell me more?"

"No," Miyake said. "I really don't."

"OK, I'll stop then. But I will say this. I think you're a good person."

"That's not the problem," Miyake said, shaking his head again. He drew a kind of design in the sand with the tip of a branch. "Tell me, Jun, have you ever thought about how you're going to die?"

Junko pondered this for a while, then shook her head.

"Well, I think about it all the time," Miyake said.

"How *are* you going to die?"

"Locked inside a refrigerator," he said. "You know. It happens all the time. Some kid is playing around inside a refrigerator that somebody's thrown away, and the door closes, and the kid suffocates. Like that."

The big log dipped to the side, scattering sparks. Miyake watched it happen but did nothing. The glow of the flames spread strangely unreal shadows across his face.

"I'm in this tight space, in total darkness, and I die little by little. It might not be so bad if I could just suffocate. But it doesn't work that way. A tiny bit of air manages to get in through some crack, so it takes a really long time. I scream, but nobody can hear me. And nobody notices I'm missing. It's so cramped in there, I can't move. I squirm and squirm but the door won't open."

Junko said nothing.

"I have the same dream over and over. I wake up in the middle of the night drenched in sweat. I've been dreaming about dying slowly in pitch-blackness, but even after I wake up, the dream doesn't end. This is the scariest part of the dream. I open my eyes, and my throat is absolutely dry. I go to the kitchen and open the refrigerator. Of course, I don't *have* a refrigerator, so I ought to realize it's a dream, but I still don't notice. I'm thinking there's something strange going on, but I open the door. Inside, the refrigerator is pitch-dark. The light's out. I wonder if there's been a power failure and stick my head inside. Hands shoot out from the darkness and grab me by the neck. Cold hands. Dead people's hands. They're incredibly strong and they start dragging me inside. I let out a huge scream, and this time I wake up for real. That's my dream. It's always the same. Always. Every little detail. And every time I have it, it's just as scary as the last."

Miyake poked the big log with the tip of a branch and pushed it back in place.

"It's so real, I feel as if I've already died hundreds of times."

"When did you start having the dream?"

"Way, way back there. So long ago I can't remember when," Miyake said. "I *have* had periods when it's left me alone. A year . . . no, two years when I didn't have it at all. I had the feeling things were going to be OK for me. But no. The dream came back. Just as I was beginning to think, I'm OK now, I'm saved, it started up again. And once it gets going, there's nothing I can do."

Miyake shook his head.

"I'm sorry, Jun, I really shouldn't be telling *you* these dark stories."

"Yes you should," Junko said. She put a cigarette between her lips and struck a match, inhaling a deep lungful of smoke. "Go on."

The bonfire was nearing its end. The big pile of extra driftwood was gone now. Miyake had thrown it all into the fire. Maybe she was imagining things, but Junko thought the ocean sounded louder.

"There's this American writer called Jack London," Miyake began.

"Sure, the guy who wrote about the fire."

"That's him. For a long time, he thought he was going to die by drowning in the sea. He was absolutely sure of it. He'd slip and fall into the ocean at night, and nobody would notice, and he'd drown."

"Did he really drown?"

Miyake shook his head. "Nope. Killed himself with morphine."

"So his premonition didn't come true. Or maybe he did something to make sure it wouldn't come true."

"On the surface, at least, it looks like that," Miyake said, pausing for a moment. "But in a sense, he was right. He *did* drown alone in a dark sea. He became an alcoholic. He soaked his body in his own despair—right to the core—and he died in agony. Premonitions can stand for something else sometimes. And the thing they stand for can be a lot more intense than reality. That's the scariest thing about having a premonition. Do you see what I mean?"

Junko thought about it for a while. She did *not* see what he meant.

"I've never once thought about how I was going to die," she said. "I *can't* think about it. I don't even know how I'm going to *live.*"

Miyake gave a nod. "I know what you mean," he said. "But there's such a thing as a way of living that's guided by the way a person's going to die."

"Is that how *you're* living?" she asked.

"I'm not sure. It seems that way sometimes."

Miyake sat down next to Junko. He looked a little more wasted and older than usual. The hair over his ears was uncut and sticking out.

"What kind of pictures have you been painting?" she asked.

"That would be tough to explain."

"OK, then, what's the newest thing you've painted?"

"I call it *Landscape with Flatiron.* I finished it three days ago. It's just a picture of an iron in a room."

"Why's that so tough to explain?"

"Because it's not really an iron."

She looked up at him. "The iron is not an iron?"

"That's right."

"Meaning it stands for something else?"

"Probably."

"Meaning you can only paint it if you use something else to stand for it?"

Miyake nodded in silence.

Junko looked up to see that there were many more stars in the sky than before. The moon had covered a long distance. Miyake threw the last piece, the long branch he was holding, into the fire. Junko leaned toward him so that their shoulders were just touching. The smoky smell of a hundred fires clung to his jacket. She took in a long, deep breath of it.

"You know something?" she said.

"What?"

"I'm completely empty."

"Yeah?"

"Yeah."

She closed her eyes and, before she knew it, tears were flowing down her cheeks. With her right hand, she gripped Miyake's knee as hard as she could through his chinos. Small chills ran through her body. He put his arm around her shoulders and drew her close, but still her tears would not stop.

"There's really nothing at all in here," she said much later, her voice hoarse. "I'm cleaned out. Empty."

"I know what you mean," he said.

"Really?"

"Yeah. I'm an expert."

"What can I do?"

"Get a good night's sleep. That usually fixes it."

"What I've got is not so easy to fix."

"You may be right, Jun. It may not be that easy."

Just then a long, steamy hiss announced the evaporation of water trapped in a log. Miyake raised his eyes and, narrowing them, peered at the bonfire for a time.

"So, what should I do?" Junko asked.

"I don't know. We could die together. What do you say?"

"Sounds good to me."

"Are you serious?"

"I'm serious."

His arm still around her shoulders, Miyake kept silent for a while. Junko buried her face in the soft worn-out leather of his jacket.

"Anyhow, let's wait till the fire burns out," Miyake said. "We built it, so we ought to keep it company to the end. Once it goes out, and it turns pitch-dark, then we can die."

"Good," Junko said. "But how?"

"I'll think of something."

"OK."

Wrapped in the smell of the fire, Junko closed her eyes. Miyake's arm across her shoulders was rather small for that of a grown man, and strangely bony. I could never live with this man, she thought. I could never get inside his heart. But I might be able to die with him.

She felt herself growing sleepy. It must be the whiskey, she thought. Most of the burning driftwood had turned to ash and crumbled, but the biggest piece still glowed orange, and she could feel its gentle warmth against her skin. It would be a while before it burnt itself out.

"Mind if I take a little nap?" she asked.

"Sure, go ahead."

"Will you wake me when the fire's out?"

"Don't worry. When the fire goes out, you'll start feeling the cold. You'll wake up whether you want to or not."

She repeated the words in her mind: *When the fire goes out, you'll start feeling the cold. You'll wake up whether you want to or not.* Then she curled herself against him and dropped into a fleeting, but deep, sleep.

all god's children can dance

Yoshiya woke with the worst possible hangover. He could barely open one eye; the left lid wouldn't budge. His head felt as if it had been stuffed with decaying teeth during the night. A foul sludge was oozing from his rotting gums and eating away at his brain from the inside. If he ignored it, he wouldn't have a brain left. Which would be all right, too. Just a little more sleep: that's all he wanted. But he knew it was out of the question. He felt too awful to sleep.

He looked for the clock by his pillow, but it had vanished. Why wasn't it there? No glasses, either. He must have tossed them somewhere. It had happened before.

Got to get up. He managed to raise the upper half of his body, but this jumbled his mind, and his face plunged back into the pillow. A truck came through the neighborhood selling clothes-drying poles. They'd take your old ones and exchange them for new ones, the loudspeaker announced, and the price was the same as twenty years ago. The monotonous, stretched-out voice belonged to a middle-aged man. It made him feel queasy, but he couldn't vomit.

The best cure for a bad hangover was to watch a morning talk show, according to one friend. The shrill witch-hunter voices of the showbiz correspondents would bring up every last bit left in your stomach from the night before.

But Yoshiya didn't have the strength to drag himself to the TV. Just breathing was hard enough. Random but persistent streams of clear light and white smoke swirled together inside his eyes, which gave him a strangely flat view of the world. Was this what it felt like to die? OK. But once was enough. Please, God, never do this to me again.

"God" made him think of his mother. He started to call out to her for a glass of water, but realized he was home alone. She and the other believers had left for Kansai three days ago. It takes all kinds to make a world: a volunteer servant of God was the mother of this hangover heavyweight. He couldn't get up. He still couldn't open his left eye. Who the hell could he have been drinking so much with? No way to remember. Just trying turned the core of his brain to stone. Never mind now: he'd think about it later.

It couldn't be noon yet. But still, Yoshiya figured, judging from the glare of what seeped past the curtains, it had to be after eleven. Some degree of lateness on the part of a young staff member was never a big deal to his employer, a publishing company. He had always evened things out by working late. But showing up after noon had earned him some sharp remarks from the boss. These he could ignore, but he didn't want to cause any problems for the believer who had recommended him for the job.

It was almost one o'clock by the time he left the house. Any other day, he would have made up an excuse and stayed home, but he had one document on disk that he had to format and print out today, and it was not a job that anyone else could do.

He left the condo in Asagaya that he rented with his mother, took the elevated Chuo Line to Yotsuya, transferred to the Marunouchi Line subway, took that as far as Kasumigaseki, transferred again, this time to the Hibiya Line subway, and got off at Kamiya-cho, the station closest to the small foreign travel guide publishing company where he worked. He climbed up and down the long flights of stairs at each station on wobbly legs.

He saw the man with the missing earlobe as he was transferring back the other way underground at Kasumigaseki around ten o'clock that night. Hair half gray, the man was somewhere in his mid-fifties: tall, no glasses, old-fashioned tweed overcoat, briefcase in right hand. He walked with the slow pace of someone deep in thought, heading from the Hibiya Line platform toward the Chiyoda Line. Without hesitation, Yoshiya fell in after him. That's when he noticed that his throat was as dry as a piece of old leather.

Yoshiya's mother was forty-three, but she didn't look more than thirty-five. She had clean, classic good looks, a great figure that she preserved with a simple diet and vigorous workouts morning and evening, and dewy skin. Only eighteen years older than Yoshiya, she was often taken for his elder sister.

She had never had much in the way of maternal instincts, or perhaps she was just eccentric. Even after Yoshiya had entered middle school and begun to take an interest in things sexual, she would continue to walk around the house wearing skimpy underwear—or nothing at all. They slept in separate bedrooms, of course, but whenever she felt lonely at night she would crawl under his covers with almost nothing on. As if hugging a dog or cat, she would sleep with an arm thrown over Yoshiya, who knew she meant nothing by it, but still it made him nervous. He would have to twist himself into incredible positions to keep his mother unaware of his erection.

Terrified of stumbling into a fatal relationship with his own mother, Yoshiya embarked on a frantic search for an easy lay. As long as one failed to materialize, he would take care to masturbate at regular intervals. He even went so far as to patronize a porn shop while he was still in high school, using the money he made from part-time jobs.

He should have left his mother's house and begun living on his own, Yoshiya knew, and he had wrestled with the question at critical moments—when he entered college and again when he took a job. But here he was, twenty-five years old, and still unable to tear himself away. One reason for this, he felt, was that there was no telling what his mother might do if he were to leave her alone. He had devoted vast amounts of energy over the years to preventing her from carrying out the wild, self-destructive (albeit good-hearted) schemes that she was always coming up with.

Plus, there was bound to be a terrible outburst if he were to announce all of a sudden that he was leaving home. He was sure it had never once crossed his mother's mind that they might someday live apart. He recalled all too vividly her profound heartbreak and distress when he announced at the age of thirteen that he was abandoning the faith. For two solid weeks or more she ate nothing, said nothing, never once took a bath or combed her hair or changed her underwear. She only just managed to attend to her period when it came. Yoshiya had never seen his mother in such a filthy, smelly state. Just imagining its happening again gave him chest pains.

Yoshiya had no father. From the time he was born there had been only his mother, and she had told him again and again when he was a little boy, "Your father is our Lord" (which is how they referred to their god). "Our Lord must stay high up in Heaven; He can't live down here with us. But He is always watching over you, Yoshiya, He always has your best interests at heart."

Mr. Tabata, who served as little Yoshiya's special "guide," would say the same kinds of things to him:

"It's true, you do not have a father in this world, and you're going to meet all sorts of people who say stupid things to you about that. Unfortunately, the eyes of most people are clouded and unable to see the truth, Yoshiya, but Our Lord, your father, *is* the world itself. You are fortunate to live in the embrace of His love. You must be proud of that and live a life that is good and true."

"I know," responded Yoshiya just after he had entered elementary school. "But God belongs to everybody, doesn't He? Fathers are different, though. Everybody has a different one. Isn't that right?"

"Listen to me, Yoshiya. Someday our Lord, your father, will reveal Himself to you as yours and yours alone. You will meet

Him when and where you least expect it. But if you begin to doubt or to abandon your faith, He may be so disappointed that He never shows Himself to you. Do you understand?"

"I understand."

"And you will keep in mind what I've said to you?"

"I will keep it in mind, Mr. Tabata."

But in fact what Mr. Tabata told him did not make much sense to Yoshiya because he could not believe that he was a special "child of God." He was ordinary, just like the other boys and girls he saw everywhere—or perhaps he was even a little bit less than ordinary. He had nothing that helped him to stand out, and he was always making a mess of things. It was like that all through elementary school. His grades were decent enough, but when it came to sports he was hopeless. He had slow and spindly legs, myopic eyes, and clumsy hands. In baseball, he missed most fly balls that came his way. His teammates would grumble, and the girls in the stands would titter.

Yoshiya would pray to God, his father, each night before bedtime: "I promise to maintain unwavering faith in You if only You will let me catch outfield flies. That's all I ask (for now)." If God really *was* his father, He should be able to do that much for him. But his prayer was never answered. The flies continued to drop from his glove.

"This means you are *testing* our Lord, Yoshiya," said Mr. Tabata sternly. "There is nothing wrong with praying for something, but you must pray for something grander than that. It is wrong to pray for something concrete, with time limits."

When Yoshiya turned seventeen, his mother revealed the secret of his birth (more or less). He was old enough to know the truth, she said.

"I was living in a deep darkness in my teen years. My soul was in chaos as deep as a newly formed ocean of mud. The true light was hidden behind dark clouds. And so I *had knowledge* of several different men without love. You know what it means to *have knowledge*, don't you?"

Yoshiya said that he did indeed know what it meant. His mother used incredibly old-fashioned language when it came to sexual matters. By that point in his life, he himself had *had knowledge* of several different girls without love.

His mother continued her story. "I first became pregnant in the second year of high school. At the time, I had no idea how very much it meant to become pregnant. A friend of mine introduced me to a doctor who gave me an abortion. He was a very kind man, and very young, and after the operation he lectured me on contraception. Abortion was good neither for the body nor the spirit, he said, and I should also be careful about venereal disease, so I should always be sure to use a condom, and he gave me a new box of them.

"I told him that I *had* used condoms, so he said, 'Well, then someone didn't put them on right. It's amazing how few people know the right way to use them.' But I'm not stupid. I was being very careful about contraception. The minute we took our clothes off, I would be sure to put it on the man myself. You can't trust men with something like that. You know about condoms, right?"

Yoshiya said that he did know about condoms.

"So, two months later I got pregnant again. I could hardly believe it: I was being more careful than ever. There was nothing I could do but go back to the same doctor. He took one look at me and said, 'I *told* you to be careful. What have you got in that head of yours?' I couldn't stop crying. I explained to him how much care I had taken with contraception whenever I *had knowledge*, but he wouldn't believe me. 'This would never have happened if you'd put them on right,' he said. He was *mad*.

"Well, to make a long story short, about six months later, because of a weird sequence of events, I ended up having knowledge of the doctor himself. He was thirty at the time, and still a bachelor. He was kind of boring to talk to, but he was a decent, honest man. His right earlobe was missing. A dog chewed it off when he was a boy. He was just walking along the street one day when a big black dog he had never seen before jumped on him and bit off his earlobe. He used to say he was glad it was just an earlobe. You could live without an earlobe. But a nose would be different. I had to agree with him.

"Being with him helped me get my old self back. When I was having knowledge of him, I managed not to think disturbing thoughts. I even got to like his little ear. He was so dedicated to his work he would lecture me on the use of the condom while we were in bed—like, when and how to put it on and when and how to take it off. You'd think this would make for foolproof contraception, but I ended up pregnant again."

Yoshiya's mother went to see her doctor lover and told him she seemed to be pregnant. He examined her and confirmed that it was so. But he would not admit to being the father. "I am a professional," he said. "My contraceptive techniques are beyond reproach. Which means you must have had relations with another man."

"This really hurt me. He made me *so* angry when he said that, I couldn't stop shaking. Can you see how deeply this would have hurt me?"

Yoshiya said that he did see.

"While I was with him, I never had knowledge of another man. Not once. But he just thought of me as some kind of slut. That was the last I saw of him. I didn't have an abortion, either. I decided to kill myself. And I would have. I would have gotten on a boat to Oshima and thrown myself from the deck if Mr. Tabata hadn't seen me wandering down the street and spoken to me. I wasn't the least bit afraid to die. Of course, if I *had* died then, *you* would never have been born into this world, Yoshiya. But thanks to Mr. Tabata's guidance, I have become the saved person you know me as today. At last, I was able to find the true light. And with the help of the other believers, I brought you into this world."

To Yoshiya's mother, Mr. Tabata had had this to say:

"You took the most rigorous contraceptive measures, and yet you became pregnant. Indeed, you became pregnant three times in a row. Do you imagine that such a thing could happen by chance? I for one do not believe it. Three 'chance' occurrences are no longer 'chance.' The number three is none other than that which is used by our Lord for revelations. In other words, Miss Osaki, it is our Lord's wish for you to give birth to a child. The child you are carrying is not just anyone's child,

Miss Osaki: it is the child of our Lord in Heaven; a male child, and I shall give it the name of Yoshiya, 'For it is good.'"

And when, as Mr. Tabata predicted, a boy child was born, they named him Yoshiya, and Yoshiya's mother lived as the servant of God, no longer having knowledge of any man.

"So," Yoshiya said, with some hesitation, to his mother, "biologically speaking, my father is that obstetrician that you . . . *had knowledge* of."

"Not true!" declared his mother with eyes blazing. "His contraceptive methods were absolutely foolproof! Mr. Tabata was right: your father is our Lord. You came into this world not through carnal knowledge but through an act of our Lord's will!"

His mother's faith was absolute, but Yoshiya was just as certain that his father was the obstetrician. There had been something wrong with the condom. Anything else was out of the question.

"Does the doctor know that you gave birth to me?"

"I don't think so," his mother said. "I never saw him again, never contacted him in any way. He probably has no idea."

The man boarded the Chiyoda Line train to Abiko. Yoshiya followed him into the car. It was after ten-thirty at night, and there were few other passengers on the train. The man took a seat and pulled a magazine from his briefcase. It looked like some sort of professional journal. Yoshiya sat down opposite and pretended to read his newspaper. The man had a slim build and deeply chiseled features with an earnest expression. There was something doctorish about him. His age looked right, and he was missing one earlobe. The right one. It could easily have been bitten off by a dog.

Yoshiya felt with intuitive certainty that this man had to be his biological father. And yet the man probably had no idea that this son of his even existed. Nor would he be likely to accept the facts if Yoshiya were to reveal them to him there and then. After all, the doctor was a professional whose contraceptive methods were beyond reproach.

The train passed through the Shin-Ochanomizu, Sendagi, and Machiya subway stops before rising to the surface. The number of passengers decreased at each station. The man never looked away from his magazine or gave any indication he was about to leave his seat. Observing him over the top of his newspaper, Yoshiya recalled fragments of the night before. He had gone out drinking in Roppongi with an old college friend and two girls the friend knew. He remembered going from the bar to a club, but he couldn't recall whether he had slept with his date. Probably not, he decided. He had been too drunk: *knowledge* would have been out of the question.

The paper was filled with the usual earthquake stories. Meanwhile his mother and the other believers were probably staying in the church's Osaka facility. Each morning they would cram their rucksacks full of supplies, travel as far as they could by commuter train, then walk along the rubble-strewn highway the rest of the way to Kobe, where they would distribute daily provisions to the victims of the quake. She had told him on the phone that her pack weighed as much as thirty-five pounds. Kobe felt light-years away from Yoshiya and the man sitting across from him absorbed in his magazine.

———

Until he graduated from elementary school, Yoshiya used to go out with his mother once a week on missionary work. She achieved the best results of anyone in the church. She was so young and lovely and seemingly well bred (in fact, she *was* well bred) that people always liked her. Plus she had this charming little boy with her. Most people would let down their guard in her presence. They might not be interested in religion, but they were willing to listen to her. She would go from house to house in a simple (but form-fitting) suit distributing pamphlets and calmly extolling the joys of faith.

"Be sure to come see us if you ever have any pain or difficulties," she would tell them. "We never push, we only offer," she would add, her voice warm, eyes shining. "There was a time when my soul was wandering through the deepest darkness until the day I was saved by our teachings. I was carrying this child inside me, and I was about to throw myself and him in the ocean. But I was saved by His hand, the One who is in Heaven, and now my son and I live in the holy light of our Lord."

Yoshiya had never found it embarrassing to knock on strangers' doors with his mother. She was especially sweet to him then, her hand always warm. They had the experience of being turned away so often that it made Yoshiya all the more joyful to receive a rare kind word. And when they managed to win over a new believer for the church it filled him with pride. Maybe now God my father will recognize me as His son, he would think.

Not long after he went on to middle school, though, Yoshiya

abandoned his faith. As he awakened to the existence of his own independent ego, he found it increasingly difficult to accept the strict codes of the sect that clashed with ordinary values. But the most fundamental and decisive cause was the unending coldness of the One who was his father: His dark, heavy, silent heart of stone. Yoshiya's abandonment of the faith was a source of deep sadness to his mother, but his determination was unshakable.

The train was almost out of Tokyo and just a station or two from crossing into Chiba Prefecture when the man put his magazine back into his briefcase and stood up, approaching the door. Yoshiya followed him on to the platform. The man flashed a pass to get through the gate, but Yoshiya had to wait in line to pay the extra fare to this distant point. Still, he managed to reach the line for cabs just as the man was stepping into one. He boarded the next cab and pulled a brand-new ten-thousand-yen bill from his wallet.

"Follow that cab," he said.

The driver gave him a suspicious look, then eyed the money.

"Hey, is this some kind of mob thing?"

"Don't worry," Yoshiya said. "I'm just tailing somebody."

The driver took the ten-thousand-yen bill and pulled away from the curb. "OK," he said, "but I still want my fare. The meter's running."

The two cabs sped down a block of shuttered shops, past a number of dark empty lots, past the lighted windows of a hospital, and through a new development crammed with boxy little houses. The streets all but empty, the tail posed no problems—

and provided no thrills. Yoshiya's driver was clever enough to vary the distance between his cab and the one in front.

"Guy havin' an affair or something?"

"Nah," Yoshiya said. "Head-hunting. Two companies fighting over one guy."

"No kidding? I knew companies were scramblin' for people these days, but I didn't realize it was this bad."

Now there were hardly any houses along the road, which followed a riverbank and entered an area lined with factories and warehouses. The only things marking this deserted space were new lampposts thrusting up from the earth. Where a high concrete wall stretched along the road, the taxi ahead came to a sudden stop. Alerted by the car's brake lights, Yoshiya's driver brought his cab to a halt some hundred yards behind the other vehicle and doused his headlights. The mercury vapor lamps overhead cast their harsh glare on the asphalt roadway. There was nothing to see here but the wall and its dense crown of barbed wire that seemed to defy the rest of the world. Far ahead, the cab door opened and the man with the missing earlobe got out. Yoshiya slipped his driver two thousand-yen bills beyond his initial ten-thousand-yen payment.

"You're never gonna get a cab way out here, mister. Want me to wait around?" the driver asked.

"Never mind," Yoshiya said and stepped outside.

The man never looked up after leaving his cab but walked straight ahead alongside the concrete wall at the same slow, steady pace as on the subway platform. He looked like a well-made mechanical doll being drawn ahead by a magnet. Yoshiya raised his coat collar and exhaled an occasional white cloud of breath from the gap between the edges as he followed the man, keeping far enough behind to avoid being spotted. All he could hear was the anonymous slapping of the man's leather shoes against the pavement. Yoshiya's rubber-soled loafers were silent.

There was no sign of human life here. The place looked like an imaginary stage set in a dream. Where the concrete wall ended, there was a scrap yard: a hill of cars surrounded by a chain-link fence. Under the flat light of a mercury lamp, the pile of withered metal was reduced to a single colorless mass. The man continued walking straight ahead.

Yoshiya wondered what the point could be of getting out of a cab in such a deserted place. Wasn't the man heading home? Or maybe he wanted to take a little detour on the way. The February night was too cold for walking, though. A freezing wind would push against Yoshiya's back every now and then as it sliced down the road.

Where the scrap yard ended, another long stretch of un-friendly concrete wall began, broken only by the opening to a narrow alley. This seemed like familiar territory to the man: he never hesitated as he turned the corner. The alley was dark. Yoshiya could make out nothing in its depths. He hesitated for a moment, but then stepped in after the man. Having come this far, he was not about to give up.

High walls pressed in on either side of the straight passage-way. There was barely enough room in here for two people to pass each other, and it was as dark as the bottom of the night-time sea. Yoshiya had only the sound of the man's shoes to go by. The leather slaps continued on ahead of him at the same unbroken pace. All but clinging to the sound, Yoshiya moved forward through this world devoid of light. And then there was no sound at all.

Had the man sensed he was being followed? Was he standing still now, holding his breath, straining to see and hear what was behind him? Yoshiya's heart shrank in the darkness, but he swallowed its loud beating and pressed on. To hell with it, he thought. So what if he screams at me for following him? I'll just tell him the truth. It could be the quickest way to set the record straight. But then the alley came to a dead end, where it was closed off by a sheet-metal fence. Yoshiya took a few seconds to find the gap, an opening just big enough to let a person through where someone had bent back the metal. He gathered the skirts of his coat around him and squeezed through.

A big open space spread out on the other side of the fence. It was no empty lot, though, but some kind of playing field. Yoshiya stood there, straining to see anything in the pale moonlight. The man was gone.

Yoshiya was standing in a baseball field, somewhere way out in center field amid a stretch of trampled-down weeds. Bare ground showed through like a scar in the one place where the center fielder usually stood. Over the distant home plate, the backstop soared like a set of black wings. The pitcher's mound lay closer to hand, a slight swelling of the earth. The high metal fence ringed the entire outfield. A breeze swept across the grass, carrying an empty potato chip bag with it to nowhere.

Yoshiya plunged his hands into his coat pockets and held his breath, waiting for something to happen. But nothing happened. He surveyed right field, then left field, then the pitcher's mound and the ground beneath his feet before looking up at the sky. Several chunks of cloud hung there, the moon tinging their hard edges a strange color. A whiff of dog shit mixed with the smell of the grass. The man had disappeared without a trace. If Mr. Tabata had been here, he would have said, "So you see, Yoshiya, our Lord reveals Himself to us in the most unexpected forms." But Mr. Tabata was dead.

He had died of urethral cancer three years ago. His final months of suffering were excruciating to see. Had he never once in all that time tested God? Had he never once prayed to God for some small relief from his terrible pain? Mr. Tabata had observed his own strict commandments with such rigor and lived in such intimate contact with God that he of all people was qualified to make such prayers (concrete and limited in time though they might be). And besides, thought Yoshiya, if it was all right for God to test man, why was it wrong for man to test God?

Yoshiya felt a faint throbbing in his temples, but he could not tell if this was the remains of his hangover or something else. With a grimace, he pulled his hands from his pockets and began taking long, slow strides toward home base. Only seconds earlier, the one thing on his mind had been the breathless pursuit of a man who might well be his father, and that had carried him to this ball field in a neighborhood he'd never seen before. Now that the stranger had disappeared, however, the importance of the succeeding acts that had brought him this far turned unclear inside him. Meaning itself broke down and would never be the same again, just as the question of whether he could catch an outfield fly had ceased to be a matter of life and death to him anymore.

What was I hoping to gain from this? he asked himself as he strode ahead. Was I trying to confirm the ties that make it possible for me to exist here and now? Was I hoping to be woven into some new plot, to be given some new and better-defined role to play? No, he thought, that's not it. What I was chasing in circles must have been the tail of the darkness inside me. I just happened to catch sight of it, and followed it, and clung to it, and in the end let it fly into still deeper darkness. I'm sure I'll never see it again.

Yoshiya's spirit now lingered in the stillness and clarity of one particular point in time and space. So what if the man was his father, or God, or some stranger who just happened to have lost his right earlobe? It no longer made any difference to him, and this in itself had been a manifestation, a sacrament: should he be singing words of praise?

He climbed the pitcher's mound and, standing on its worn footrest, stretched himself to his full height. He intertwined his fingers, thrust his arms aloft and, sucking in a lungful of cold night air, looked up once more at the moon. It was huge. Why was the moon so big one day and so small another? Simple plank bleachers ran the length of the first- and third-base lines. Empty, of course: it was the middle of a February night. Three levels of straight plank seats ascended in long, chilly rows. Windowless, gloomy buildings—some kind of warehouses, probably—huddled together beyond the backstop. No light. No sound.

Standing on the mound, Yoshiya swung his arms up, over, and down in large circles. He moved his feet in time with this, forward and to the side. As he went on with these dancelike motions, his body began to warm and to recover the full senses of a living organism. Before long he realized that his headache was all but gone.

Yoshiya's girlfriend throughout his college years called him "Super-Frog" because he looked like some kind of giant frog when he danced. She loved to dance and would always drag him out to clubs. "Look at you!" she used to say. "I love the way you flap those long arms and legs of yours! You're like a frog in the rain!"

This hurt the first time she said it, but after he had gone with her long enough, Yoshiya began to enjoy dancing. As he let himself go and moved his body in time to the music, he would come to feel that the natural rhythm inside him was pulsing in perfect unison with the basic rhythm of the world. The ebb and flow of the tide, the dancing of the wind across the plains, the course of the stars through the heavens: he felt certain that these things were by no means occurring in places unrelated to him.

She had never seen a penis as huge as his, his girlfriend used to say, taking hold of it. Didn't it get in the way when he danced? No, he would tell her: it never got in the way. True, he had a big one. It had always been on the big side, from the time he was a boy. He could not recall that it had ever been of any great advantage to him, though. In fact, several girls had refused to have sex with him because it was *too* big. In aesthetic terms, it just looked slow and clumsy and stupid. Which is why he always tried to keep it hidden. "Your big wee-wee is a sign," his mother used to tell him with absolute conviction. "It shows that you're the child of God." And he believed it, too. But then one day the craziness of it struck him. All he had ever prayed for was the ability to catch outfield flies, in answer to which God had bestowed upon him a penis that was bigger than anybody else's. What kind of world came up with such idiotic bargains?

Yoshiya took off his glasses and slipped them into their case. Dancing, huh? Not a bad idea. Not bad at all. He closed his eyes and, feeling the white light of the moon on his skin, began to dance all by himself. He drew his breath deep into his lungs and exhaled just as deeply. Unable to think of a song to match his mood, he danced in time with the stirring of the grass and the flowing of the clouds. Before long, he began to feel that someone, somewhere, was watching him. His whole body—his skin, his bones—told him with absolute certainty that he was in *someone's* field of vision. So what? he thought. Let them look if they want to, whoever they are. All God's children can dance.

He trod the earth and whirled his arms, each graceful movement calling forth the next in smooth, unbroken links, his body tracing diagrammatic patterns and impromptu variations, with invisible rhythms behind and between rhythms. At each crucial point in his dance, he could survey the complex intertwining of these elements. Animals lurked in the forest like trompe l'oeil figures, some of them horrific beasts he had never seen before. He would eventually have to pass through the forest, but he felt no fear. Of course—the forest was inside him, he knew, and it made him who he was. The beasts were ones that he himself possessed.

How long he went on dancing, Yoshiya could not tell. But it was long enough for him to perspire under the arms. And then it struck him what lay buried far down under the earth on which his feet were so firmly planted: the ominous rumbling of the deepest darkness, secret rivers that transported desire, slimy creatures writhing, the lair of earthquakes ready to transform whole cities into mounds of rubble. These, too, were helping to create the rhythm of the earth. He stopped dancing and, catching his breath, stared at the ground beneath his feet as though peering into a bottomless hole.

He thought of his mother far away in that ruined city. What would happen, he wondered, if he could remain his present self and yet turn time backward so as to meet his mother in her youth when her soul was in its deepest state of darkness? No doubt they would plunge as one into the muck of bedlam and devour each other in acts for which they would be dealt the harshest punishment. And what of it? "Punishment"? I was due for punishment long ago. The city should have crumbled to bits around me long ago.

His girlfriend had asked him to marry her when they graduated from college. "I want to be married to you, Super-Frog. I want to live with you and have your child—a boy, with a big thing just like yours."

"I can't marry you," Yoshiya said. "I know I should have told you this, but I'm the son of God. I can't marry anybody."

"Is that true?"

"It is. I'm sorry."

He knelt down and scooped up a handful of sand which he sifted through his fingers back to earth. He did this again and again. The chilly, uneven touch of the soil reminded him of the last time he had held Mr. Tabata's emaciated hand.

"I won't be alive much longer, Yoshiya," Mr. Tabata said in a voice that had grown hoarse. Yoshiya began to protest, but Mr. Tabata stopped him with a gentle shake of the head.

"Never mind," he said. "This life is nothing but a short, painful dream. Thanks to His guidance, I have made it through this far. Before I die, though, there is one thing I have to tell you. It shames me to say it, but I have no choice: I have had lustful thoughts toward your mother any number of times. As you well know, I have a family that I love with all my heart, and your mother is a pure-hearted person, but still, I have had violent cravings for her flesh—cravings that I have never been able to suppress. I want to beg your forgiveness."

There is no need for you to beg anyone's forgiveness, Mr. Tabata. You are not the only one who has had lustful thoughts. Even I, her son, have been pursued by terrible obsessions . . . Yoshiya wanted to open himself up in this way, but he knew that all it would accomplish would be to upset Mr. Tabata even more. He took Mr. Tabata's hand and held it for a very long time, hoping that the thoughts in his breast would communicate themselves from his hand to Mr. Tabata's. Our hearts are not stones. A stone may disintegrate in time and lose its outward form. But hearts never disintegrate. They have no outward form, and whether good or evil, we can always communicate them to one another. All God's children can dance. The next day, Mr. Tabata drew his last breath.

Kneeling on the pitcher's mound, Yoshiya gave himself up to the flow of time. Somewhere in the distance he heard the faint wail of a siren. A gust of wind set the leaves of grass to dancing and celebrated the grass's song before it died.

"Oh God," Yoshiya said aloud.

thailand

There was an announcement: *Lettuce angel men. We aren't countering some tah bulence. Please retahn to yah seat at thees time and fasten yah seat belt.* Satsuki had been letting her mind wander, and so it took her a while to decipher the Thai steward's shaky Japanese.

She was hot and sweating. It was like a steam bath, her whole body aflame, her nylons and bra so uncomfortable she wanted to fling everything off and set herself free. She craned her neck to see the other business-class passengers. No, she was obviously the only one suffering from the heat. They were all curled up, asleep, blankets around their shoulders to counter the air-conditioning. It must be another hot flash. Satsuki bit her lip and decided to concentrate on something else to forget about the heat. She opened her book and tried to read from where she had left off, but forgetting was out of the question. This was no ordinary heat. And they wouldn't be touching down in Bangkok for hours yet. She asked a passing stewardess for some water and, finding the pill case in her pocketbook, she washed down a dose of the hormones she had forgotten to take.

Menopause: it had to be the gods' ironic warning to (or just plain nasty trick on) humanity for having artificially extended the life span, she told herself for the nth time. A mere hundred years ago, the average life span was less than fifty, and any woman who went on living twenty or thirty years past the end of her menstruation was an oddity. The difficulty of continuing to live with tissues for which the ovaries or the thyroid had ceased to secrete the normal supply of hormones; the possible relationship between the postmenopausal decrease in estrogen levels and the incidence of Alzheimer's: these were not questions worth troubling one's mind over. Of far more importance to the majority of mankind was the challenge of simply obtaining enough food to eat each day. Had the advancement of medicine, then, done nothing more than to expose, subdivide, and further complicate the problems faced by the human species?

Soon another announcement came over the PA system. In English this time. *If there is a doctor on board, please identify yourself to one of the cabin attendants.*

A passenger must have taken sick. For a moment Satsuki thought of volunteering, but quickly changed her mind. On the two earlier occasions when she had done so, she had merely had run-ins with practicing physicians who happened to be on the plane. These men had seemed to possess both the poise of a seasoned general commanding troops on the front line and the vision to recognize at a glance that Satsuki was a professional pathologist without combat experience. "That's all right, Doctor," she had been told with a cool smile, "I can handle this by myself. You just take it easy." She had mumbled a stupid excuse and gone back to her seat to watch the rest of some ridiculous movie.

Still, she thought, I might just be the only doctor on this plane. And the patient might be someone with a major problem involving the thyroidal immune system. If that is the case—and the likelihood of such a situation did not seem high—then even I might be of some use. She took a breath and pressed the button for a cabin attendant.

The World Thyroid Conference was a four-day event at the Bangkok Marriott. Actually, it was more like a worldwide family reunion than a conference. All the participants were thyroid specialists, and they all knew each other or were quickly introduced. It was a small world. There would be lectures and panel discussions during the day and private parties at night. Friends would get together to renew old ties, drink Australian wine, share thyroid stories, whisper gossip, update each other on their careers, tell dirty doctor jokes, and sing "Surfer Girl" at karaoke bars.

In Bangkok, Satsuki stayed mainly with her Detroit friends. Those were the ones she felt most comfortable with. She had worked at the university hospital in Detroit for almost ten years, researching the immune function of the thyroid gland. Eventually she had had a falling-out with her securities analyst husband, whose dependency on alcohol had grown worse year by year, in addition to which he had become involved with another woman—someone Satsuki knew well. They separated, and a bitter feud involving lawyers had dragged on for a full year. "The thing that finally did it for me," her husband claimed, "was that you didn't want to have children."

They had finally concluded their divorce settlement three years ago. A few months later, someone smashed the headlights of her Honda Accord in the hospital parking lot and wrote "JAP CAR" on the hood in white letters. She called the police. A big black policeman filled out the damage report and then said to her, "Lady, this is Detroit. Next time buy a Ford Taurus."

What with one thing and another, Satsuki became fed up with living in America and decided to return to Japan. She found a position at a university hospital in Tokyo. "You can't do that," said a member of her research team from India. "All our years of research are about to bear fruit. We could be nominated for a Nobel Prize—it's not that crazy," he pleaded with her to stay, but Satsuki's mind was made up. Something inside her had snapped.

She stayed on alone at the hotel in Bangkok after the conference ended. "I've worked out a vacation for myself after this," she told her friends. "I'm going to a resort near here for a complete rest—a whole week of nothing but reading, swimming, and drinking nice cold cocktails by the pool."

"That's great," they said. "Everybody needs a breather once in a while—it's good for your thyroid, too!" With handshakes and hugs and promises to get together again, Satsuki said goodbye to all her friends.

Early the next morning, a limousine pulled up to the hotel entrance as planned. It was an old navy blue Mercedes, as perfect and polished as a jewel and far more beautiful than a new car. It looked like an object from another world, as if it had dropped fully formed from someone's fantasies. A slim Thai man probably in his early sixties was to be her driver and guide. He wore a heavily starched white short-sleeved shirt, a black silk necktie, and dark sunglasses. His face was tanned, his neck long and slender. Presenting himself to Satsuki, he did not shake her hand but instead brought his hands together and gave a slight, almost Japanese, bow.

"Please call me Nimit. I will have the honor to be your companion for the coming week."

It was not clear whether "Nimit" was his first or last name. He was, in any case, "Nimit," and he told her this in a courteous, easy-to-understand English devoid of American casualness or British affectation. He had, in fact, no perceptible accent. Satsuki had heard English spoken this way before, but she couldn't remember where.

"The honor is mine," she said.

Together, they passed through Bangkok's vulgar, noisy, polluted streets. The traffic crawled along, people cursed each other, and the sound of car horns tore through the atmosphere like an air-raid siren. Plus, there were elephants lumbering down the street—and not just one or two of them. What were elephants doing in a city like this? she asked Nimit.

"Their owners bring them from the country," he explained. "They used to use them for logging, but there was not enough work for them to survive that way. They brought their animals to the city to make money doing tricks for tourists. Now there are far too many elephants here, and that makes things very difficult for the city people. Sometimes an elephant will panic and run amok. Just the other day, a great many automobiles were damaged that way. The police try to put a stop to it, of course, but they cannot confiscate the elephants from their keepers. There would be no place to put them if they did, and the cost of feeding them would be enormous. All they can do is leave them alone."

The car eventually emerged from the city, drove onto an expressway, and headed north. Nimit took a cassette tape from the glove compartment and slipped it into the car stereo, setting the volume low. It was jazz—a tune that Satsuki recognized with some emotion.

"Do you mind turning the volume up?" she asked.

"Yes, Doctor, of course," Nimit said, making it louder. The tune was "I Can't Get Started," in exactly the same performance she had heard so often in the old days.

"Howard McGhee on trumpet, Lester Young on tenor," she murmured, as if to herself. "JATP."

Nimit glanced at her in the rearview mirror. "Very impressive, Doctor," he said. "Do you like jazz?"

"My father was crazy about it," she said. "He played records for me when I was a little girl, the same ones over and over, and he had me memorize the performers. If I got them right, he'd give me candy. I still remember most of them. But just the old stuff. I don't know anything about the newer jazz musicians. Lionel Hampton, Bud Powell, Earl Hines, Harry Edison, Buck Clayton . . ."

"The old jazz is all I ever listen to as well," Nimit said. "What was your father's profession?"

"He was a doctor, too," she said. "A pediatrician. He died just after I entered high school."

"I am sorry to hear that," Nimit said. "Do you still listen to jazz?"

Satsuki shook her head. "Not really. Not for years. My husband hated jazz. All he liked was opera. We had a great stereo in the house, but he'd give me a sour look if I ever tried putting on anything besides opera. Opera lovers may be the narrowest people in the world. I left my husband, though. I don't think I'd mind if I never heard another opera again for as long as I live."

Nimit gave a little nod but said nothing. Hands on the Mercedes steering wheel, he stared silently at the road ahead. His technique with the steering wheel was almost beautiful, the way he would move his hands to exactly the same points on the wheel at exactly the same angle. Now Erroll Garner was playing "I'll Remember April," which brought back more memories for Satsuki. Garner's *Concert by the Sea* had been one of her father's favorite records. She closed her eyes and let herself sink into the old memories. Everything had gone well for her until her father died of cancer. Everything—without exception. But then the stage suddenly turned dark, and by the time she noticed that her father had vanished forever from her life, everything was headed in the wrong direction. It was as if a whole new story had started with a whole new plot. Barely a month had passed after her father's death when her mother sold the big stereo along with his jazz collection.

"Where are you from in Japan, Doctor, if you don't mind my asking?"

"I'm from Kyoto," answered Satsuki. "I only lived there until I was eighteen, though, and I've hardly ever been back."

"Isn't Kyoto right next to Kobe?"

"It's not too far, but not 'right next to' Kobe. At least the earthquake seems not to have caused too much damage there."

Nimit switched to the passing lane, slipping past a number of trucks loaded with livestock, then eased back into the cruising lane.

"I'm glad to hear it," Nimit said. "A lot of people died in the earthquake last month. I saw it on the news. It was very sad. Tell me, Doctor, did you know anyone living in Kobe?"

"No, no one. I don't think anyone I know lives in Kobe," she said. But this was not true. *He* lived in Kobe.

Nimit remained silent for a while. Then, bending his neck slightly in her direction, he said, "Strange and mysterious things, though, aren't they—earthquakes? We take it for granted that the earth beneath our feet is solid and stationary. We even talk about people being 'down to earth' or having their feet firmly planted on the ground. But suddenly one day we see that it isn't true. The earth, the boulders, that are supposed to be so solid, all of a sudden turn as mushy as liquid. I heard it on the TV news: 'liquefaction,' they call it, I think. Fortunately we rarely have major earthquakes here in Thailand."

Cradled in the rear seat, Satsuki closed her eyes and concentrated on Erroll Garner's playing. Yes, she thought, *he* lived in Kobe. I hope he was crushed to death by something big and heavy. Or swallowed up by the liquefied earth. *It's everything I've wanted for him all these years.*

———

The limousine reached its destination at three o'clock in the afternoon. They had taken a break at a service area along the highway at precisely twelve o'clock. Satsuki had drunk some gritty coffee and eaten half a donut at the cafeteria. Her week-long rest was to be spent at an expensive resort in the mountains. The buildings overlooked a stream that surged through the valley, the slopes of which were covered in gorgeous primary-colored flowers. Birds flew from tree to tree emitting sharp cries. A private cottage had been prepared for Satsuki's stay. It had a big bright bathroom, an elegant canopy bed, and twenty-four-hour room service. Books and CDs and videos were available at the library off the lobby. The place was immaculate. Great care—and a great deal of money—had been lavished on every detail.

"You must be very tired, Doctor, after the long trip," Nimit said. "You can relax now. I will come to pick you up at ten o'clock tomorrow morning and take you to the pool. All you need to bring is a towel and bathing suit."

"Pool?" she asked. "They must have a perfectly big pool here at the hotel, don't they? At least that's what I was told."

"Yes, of course, but the hotel pool is very crowded. Mr. Rapaport told me that you are a serious swimmer. I found a pool nearby where you can do laps. There will be a charge, of course, but a small one. I'm sure you will like it."

John Rapaport was the American friend who had made the arrangements for Satsuki's Thai vacation. He had worked all over Southeast Asia as a news correspondent ever since the

Khmer Rouge had run rampant in Cambodia, and he had many connections in Thailand as well. It was he who had recommended Nimit as Satsuki's guide and driver. With a mischievous wink, he had said to her, "You won't have to think about a thing. Just shut up and let Nimit make all the decisions and everything will go perfectly. He's a very impressive guy."

"That's fine," she said to Nimit. "I'll leave it up to you."

"Well then, I will come for you at ten o'clock tomorrow . . ."

Satsuki opened her bags, smoothed the wrinkles in a dress and skirt, and hung them in the closet. Then, changing into a swimsuit, she went to the hotel pool. Just as Nimit had said, it was not a pool for serious swimming. Gourd-shaped, it had a lovely waterfall in the middle, and children were throwing a ball in the shallow area. Abandoning any thought of trying to swim, she stretched out under a parasol, ordered a Tío Pepe and Perrier, and picked up reading where she had left off in her new John le Carré novel. When she grew tired of reading, she pulled her hat down over her face and napped. She had a dream about a rabbit—a short dream. The rabbit was in a hutch surrounded by a wire-mesh fence, trembling. It seemed to be sensing the arrival of some kind of thing in the middle of the night. At first, Satsuki was observing the rabbit from outside its enclosure, but soon she herself had become the rabbit. She could just barely make out the thing in the darkness. Even after she awoke, she had a bad taste in her mouth.

He lived in Kobe. She knew his home address and telephone number. She had never once lost track of him. She had tried calling his house just after the earthquake, but the connection never went through. I hope the damn place was flattened, she thought.

I hope the whole family is out wandering through the streets, penniless. When I think of what you did to my life, when I think of the children I should have had, it's the least you deserve.

The pool that Nimit had found was half an hour's drive from the hotel and involved crossing a mountain. The woods near the top of the mountain were full of gray monkeys. They sat lined up along the road, eyes fixed on the passing cars as if to read the fates of the speeding vehicles.

The pool was inside a large, somewhat mysterious compound surrounded by a high wall and entered through an imposing iron gate. Nimit lowered his window and identified himself to the guard, who opened the gate without a word. Down the gravel driveway stood an old stone two-story building, and behind that was the long, narrow pool. Its signs of age were unmistakable, but this was an authentic three-lane, twenty-five-meter lap pool. The rectangular stretch of water was beautiful, surrounded by lawn and trees, and undisturbed by swimmers. Several old wooden deck chairs were lined up beside the pool. Silence ruled the area, and there was no hint of a human presence.

"What do you think, Doctor?" Nimit asked.

"Wonderful," Satsuki said. "Is this an athletic club?"

"Something like that," he said. "But hardly anyone uses it now. I have arranged for you to swim here alone as much as you like."

"Why, thank you so much, Nimit. You *are* an impressive man."

"You do me too great an honor," Nimit said, bowing blank-faced, with old-school courtesy. "The cottage over there is the changing room. It has toilets and showers. Feel free to use all the facilities. I will station myself by the automobile. Please let me know if there is anything you need."

Satsuki had always loved swimming, and she went to the gym pool whenever she had a chance. She had learned proper form from a coach. While she swam, she was able to thrust all unpleasant memories from her mind. If she swam long enough, she could reach a point where she felt utterly free, like a bird flying through the sky. Thanks to her years of regular exercise, she had never been confined to bed with an illness or sensed any physical disorder. Nor had she gained extra weight. Of course, she was not young anymore; a trim body was no longer an option. In particular, there was almost no way to avoid putting on a little extra flesh at the hips. You could ask for only so much. She wasn't trying to become a fashion model. She probably looked five years younger than her actual age, which was pretty damn good.

At noon, Nimit served her ice tea and sandwiches on a silver tray by the pool—tiny vegetable and cheese sandwiches cut into perfect little triangles.

Satsuki was amazed. "Did you make these?"

The question brought a momentary change to Nimit's expressionless face. "Not I, Doctor. I do not prepare food. I had someone make this."

Satsuki was about to ask who that someone might be when she stopped herself. John Rapaport had told her, "Just shut up and let Nimit make all the decisions and everything will go perfectly." The sandwiches were quite good. Satsuki rested after lunch. On her Walkman she listened to a tape of the Benny Goodman Sextet that Nimit had lent her, after which she continued with her book. She swam some more in the afternoon, returning to the hotel at three.

Satsuki repeated exactly the same routine for five days in a row. She swam to her heart's content, ate vegetable and cheese sandwiches, listened to music, and read. She never stepped out of the hotel except to go to the pool. What she wanted was perfect rest, a chance not to *think* about anything.

She was the only one using the pool. The water was always freezing cold, as if it had been drawn from an underground stream in the hills, and the first dunk always took her breath away, but a few laps would warm her up, and then the water temperature was just right. When she tired of doing the crawl, she would remove her goggles and swim backstroke. White clouds floated in the sky, and birds and dragonflies cut across them. Satsuki wished she could stay like this forever.

"Where did you learn English?" Satsuki asked Nimit on the way back from the pool.

"I worked for thirty-three years as a chauffeur for a Norwegian gem dealer in Bangkok, and I always spoke English with him."

So that explained the familiar style. One of Satsuki's colleagues at a hospital where she had worked in Baltimore, a Dane, had spoken exactly this kind of English—precise grammar, light accent, no slang. Very clean, very easy to understand, and somewhat lacking in color. How strange to be spoken to in Norwegian English in Thailand!

"My employer loved jazz. He always had a tape playing when he was in the car. Which is why, as his driver, I naturally became familiar with it as well. When he died three years ago, he left me the car and all his tapes. The one we are listening to now is one of his."

"So when he died, you became an independent driver-guide for foreigners, is that it?"

"Yes, exactly," Nimit said. "There are many driver-guides in Thailand, but I am probably the only one with his own Mercedes."

"He must have placed a great deal of trust in you."

Nimit was silent for a long time. He seemed to be searching for the right words to respond to Satsuki's remark. "You know, Doctor, I am a bachelor. I have never once married. I spent thirty-three years as another man's shadow. I went everywhere he went, I helped him with everything he did. I was in a sense a part of him. When you live like that for a long time, you gradually lose track of what it is that you yourself really want out of life."

He turned up the volume on the car stereo a little: a deep-throated tenor sax solo.

"Take this music for example. I remember exactly what he told me about it. 'Listen to this, Nimit. Follow Coleman Hawkins' improvised lines very carefully. He is using them to tell us something. Pay very close attention. He is telling us the story of the free spirit that is doing everything it can to escape from within him. That same kind of spirit is inside me, and inside you. There—you can hear it, I'm sure: the hot breath, the shiver of the heart.' Hearing the same music over and over, I learned to listen closely, to hear the sound of the spirit. But still I cannot be sure if I really did hear it with my own ears. When you are with a person for a long time and following his orders, in a sense you become one with him, like husband and wife. Do you see what I am saying, Doctor?"

"I think so," answered Satsuki.

It suddenly struck her that Nimit and his Norwegian employer might have been lovers. She had no evidence on which to base such an assumption, merely a flash of intuition. But it might explain what Nimit was trying to say.

"Still, Doctor, I do not have the slightest regret. If I could live my life over again, I would probably do exactly the same thing. What about you?"

"I don't know, Nimit. I really don't know."

Nimit said nothing after that. They crossed the mountain with the gray monkeys and returned to the hotel.

On her last day before leaving for Japan, Nimit took Satsuki to a nearby village instead of driving straight back to the hotel.

"I have a favor to ask of you," he said, meeting her eyes in the rearview mirror. "A personal favor."

"What is it?"

"Could you perhaps spare me an hour of your time? I have a place that I would like to show you."

Satsuki had no objection, nor did she ask him where he was taking her. She had decided to place herself entirely in his hands.

The woman lived in a small house at the far edge of the village—a poor house in a poor village, with one tiny rice paddy after another crammed in layers up a hillside. Filthy, emaciated livestock. Muddy, pockmarked road. Air filled with the smell

of water buffalo dung. A bull wandered by, its genitals swinging. A 50cc motorcycle buzzed past, splashing mud to either
side. Near-naked children stood lined up along the road, staring at the Mercedes. Satsuki was shocked to think that such a
miserable village could be situated so close to the high-class
resort hotel in which she was staying.

The woman was old, perhaps almost eighty. Her skin had
the blackened look of worn leather, its deep wrinkles becom-
ing ravines that seemed to travel to all parts of her body. Her
back was bent, and a flower-patterned, oversize dress hung limp
from her bony frame. When he saw her, Nimit brought his
hands together in greeting. She did the same.

Satsuki and the old woman sat down on opposite sides of a
table, and Nimit took his place at one end. At first, only the
woman and Nimit spoke. Satsuki had no idea what they were
saying to each other, but she noticed how lively and powerful
the woman's voice was for someone her age. The old woman
seemed to have a full set of teeth, too. After a while, she turned
from Nimit to face Satsuki, looking directly into her eyes. She
had a penetrating gaze, and she never blinked. Satsuki began to
feel like a small animal that has been trapped in a room with no
way to escape. She realized she was sweating all over. Her face
burned, and she had trouble breathing. She wanted to take a
pill, but she had left her bottle of mineral water in the car.

"Please put your hands on the table," Nimit said. Satsuki did
as she was told. The old woman reached out and took her right
hand. The woman's hands were small but powerful. For a full ten
minutes (though it might just as well have been two or three),
the old woman stared into Satsuki's eyes and held her hand, say-

ing nothing. Satsuki returned the woman's strong stare with her timid one, using the handkerchief in her left hand to mop her brow from time to time. Eventually, with a great sigh, the old woman released Satsuki's hand. She turned to Nimit and said something in Thai. Nimit translated into English.

"She says that there is a stone inside your body. A hard, white stone. About the size of a child's fist. She does not know where it came from."

"A stone?" Satsuki asked.

"There is something written on the stone, but she cannot read it because it is in Japanese: small black characters of some kind. The stone and its inscription are old, old things. You have been living with them inside you for a very long time. You must get rid of the stone. Otherwise, after you die and are cremated, only the stone will remain."

Now the old woman turned back to face Satsuki and spoke slowly in Thai for a long time. Her tone of voice made it clear that she was saying something important. Again Nimit translated.

"You are going to have a dream soon about a large snake. In your dream, it will be easing its way out of a hole in a wall—a green, scaly snake. Once it has pushed out three feet from the wall, you must grab its neck and never let go. The snake will look very frightening, but in fact it can do you no harm, so you must not be frightened. Hold on to it with both hands. Think of it as your life, and hold on to it with all your strength. Keep holding it until you wake from your dream. The snake will swallow your stone for you. Do you understand?"

"What in the world—?"

"Just say you understand," Nimit said with the utmost gravity.

"I understand," Satsuki said.

The old woman gave a gentle nod and spoke again to Satsuki.

"The man is not dead," translated Nimit. "He did not receive a scratch. It may not be what you wanted, but it was actually very lucky for you that he was not hurt. You should be grateful for your good fortune."

The woman uttered a few short syllables.

"That is all," Nimit said. "We can go back to the hotel now."

"Was that some kind of fortune-telling?" Satsuki asked when they were back in the car.

"No, Doctor. It was not fortune-telling. Just as you treat people's bodies, she treats people's spirits. She predicts their dreams, mostly."

"I should have left her something then, as a token of thanks. The whole thing was such a surprise to me, it slipped my mind."

Nimit negotiated a sharp curve on the mountain road, turning the wheel in that precise way of his. "I paid her," he said. "A small amount. Not enough for you to trouble yourself over. Just think of it as a mark of my personal regard for you, Doctor."

"Do you take all of your clients there?"

"No, Doctor, only you."

"And why is that?"

"You are a beautiful person, Doctor. Clearheaded. Strong. But you seem always to be dragging your heart along the ground. From now on, little by little, you must prepare yourself to face death. If you devote all of your future energy to living, you will not be able to die well. You must begin to shift gears, a little at a time. Living and dying are, in a sense, of equal value."

"Tell me something, Nimit," Satsuki said, taking off her sunglasses and leaning over the back of the passenger seat.

"What is that, Doctor?"

"Are *you* prepared to die?"

"I am half dead already," Nimit said as if stating the obvious.

That night, lying in her broad, pristine bed, Satsuki wept. She recognized that she was headed toward death. She recognized that she had a hard, white stone inside herself. She recognized that a scaly, green snake was lurking somewhere in the dark. She thought about the child to which she never gave birth. She had destroyed that child, flung it down a bottomless well. And then she had spent thirty years hating one man. She had hoped that he would die in agony. In order to bring that about, she had gone so far as to wish in the depths of her heart for an earthquake. In a sense, she told herself, I am the one who caused that earthquake. *He* turned my heart into a stone; *he* turned my body to stone. In the distant mountains, the gray monkeys were silently staring at her. *Living and dying are, in a sense, of equal value.*

After checking her bags at the airline counter, Satsuki handed Nimit an envelope containing a one-hundred-dollar bill. "Thank you for everything, Nimit. You made it possible for me to have a wonderful rest. This is a personal gift from me to you."

"That is very thoughtful of you, Doctor," said Nimit, accepting the envelope. "Thank you very much."

"Do you have time for a cup of coffee?"

"Yes, I would enjoy that."

They went to a café together. Satsuki took hers black. Nimit gave his a heavy dose of cream. For a long time, Satsuki went on turning her cup in her saucer.

"You know," she said at last, "I have a secret that I've never told anyone. I could never bring myself to talk about it. I've kept it locked up inside of me all this time. But I'd like to tell it to you now. Because we'll probably never meet again. When my father died all of a sudden, my mother, without a word to me—"

Nimit held his hands up, palms facing Satsuki, and shook his head. "Please, Doctor. Don't tell me anymore. You should have your dream, as the old woman told you to. I understand how you feel, but if you put those feelings into words they will turn into lies."

Satsuki swallowed her words, and then, in silence, closed her eyes. She drew in a full, deep breath, and let it out again.

"Have your dream, Doctor," Nimit said as if sharing kindly advice. "What you need now more than anything is discipline. Cast off mere words. Words turn into stone."

He reached out and took Satsuki's hand between his. His hands were strangely smooth and youthful, as if they had always been protected by expensive leather gloves. Satsuki opened her eyes and looked at him. Nimit took away his hands and rested them on the table, fingers intertwined.

"My Norwegian employer was actually from Lapland," he said. "You must know, of course, that Lapland is at the northernmost tip of Norway, near the North Pole. Many reindeer live there. In summer there is no night, and in winter no day. He probably came to Thailand because the cold got to be too much for him. I guess you could call the two places complete opposites. He loved Thailand, and he made up his mind to have his bones buried here. But still, to the day he died, he missed the town in Lapland where he was born. He used to tell me about it all the time. And yet, in spite of that, he never once went back to Norway in thirty-three years. Something must have happened there that kept him away. He was another person with a stone inside."

Nimit lifted his coffee cup and took a sip, then carefully set it in its saucer again without a sound.

"He once told me about polar bears—what solitary animals they are. They mate just once a year. One time in a whole year. There is no such thing as a lasting male-female bond in their world. One male polar bear and one female polar bear meet by sheer chance somewhere in the frozen vastness, and they mate. It doesn't take long. And once they are finished, the male runs away from the female as if he is frightened to death: he runs from the place where they have mated. He never looks back— literally. The rest of the year he lives in deep solitude. Mutual communication—the touching of two hearts—does not exist for them. So, that is the story of polar bears—or at least it is what my employer told me about them."

"How very strange," Satsuki said.

"Yes," Nimit said, "it *is* strange." His face was grave. "I remember asking my employer, 'Then what do polar bears exist for?' 'Yes, exactly,' he said with a big smile. 'Then what do *we* exist for, Nimit?'"

―――――

The plane reached cruising altitude and the FASTEN SEAT BELT sign went out. So, thought Satsuki, I'm going back to Japan. She tried to think about what lay ahead, but soon gave up. "Words turn into stone," Nimit had told her. She settled deep into her seat and closed her eyes. All at once the image came to her of the sky she had seen while swimming on her back. And Erroll Garner's "I'll Remember April." Let me sleep, she thought. Just let me sleep. And wait for the dream to come.

super-frog saves tokyo

Katagiri found a giant frog waiting for him in his apartment. It was powerfully built, standing over six feet tall on its hind legs. A skinny little man no more than five-foot-three, Katagiri was overwhelmed by the frog's imposing bulk.

"Call me 'Frog,'" said the frog in a clear, strong voice.

Katagiri stood rooted in the doorway, unable to speak.

"Don't be afraid, I'm not here to hurt you. Just come in and close the door. Please."

Briefcase in his right hand, grocery bag with fresh vegetables and canned salmon cradled in his left arm, Katagiri didn't dare move.

"Please, Mr. Katagiri, hurry and close the door, and take off your shoes."

The sound of his own name helped Katagiri snap out of it. He closed the door as ordered, set the grocery bag on the raised wooden floor, pinned the briefcase under one arm, and unlaced his shoes. Frog gestured for him to take a seat at the kitchen table, which he did.

"I must apologize, Mr. Katagiri, for having barged in while you were out," Frog said. "I knew it would be a shock for you to find me here. But I had no choice. How about a cup of tea? I thought you would be coming home soon, so I boiled some water."

Katagiri still had his briefcase jammed under his arm. Somebody's playing a joke on me, he thought. Somebody's rigged himself up in this huge frog costume just to have fun with me. But he knew, as he watched Frog pour boiling water into the teapot, humming all the while, that these had to be the limbs and movements of a real frog. Frog set a cup of green tea in front of Katagiri, and poured another one for himself.

Sipping his tea, Frog asked, "Calming down?"

But still Katagiri could not speak.

"I know I should have made an appointment to visit you, Mr. Katagiri. I am fully aware of the proprieties. Anyone would be shocked to find a big frog waiting for him at home. But an urgent matter brings me here. Please forgive me."

"Urgent matter?" Katagiri managed to produce words at last.

"Yes, indeed," Frog said. "Why else would I take the liberty of barging into a person's home? Such discourtesy is not my customary style."

"Does this 'matter' have something to do with me?"

"Yes and no," said Frog with a tilt of the head. "No and yes."

I've got to get a grip on myself, thought Katagiri. "Do you mind if I smoke?"

"Not at all, not at all," Frog said with a smile. "It's your home. You don't have to ask my permission. Smoke and drink as much as you like. I myself am not a smoker, but I can hardly impose my distaste for tobacco on others in their own homes."

Katagiri pulled a pack of cigarettes from his coat pocket and struck a match. He saw his hand trembling as he lit up. Seated opposite him, Frog seemed to be studying his every movement.

"You don't happen to be connected with some kind of *gang* by any chance?" Katagiri found the courage to ask.

"Ha ha ha ha ha ha! What a wonderful sense of humor you have, Mr. Katagiri!" he said, slapping his webbed hand against his thigh. "There may be a shortage of skilled labor, but what gang is going to hire a frog to do their dirty work? They'd be made a laughingstock."

"Well, if you're here to negotiate a repayment, you're wasting your time. I have no authority to make such decisions. Only my superiors can do that. I just follow orders. I can't do a thing for you."

"Please, Mr. Katagiri," Frog said, raising one webbed finger. "I have not come here on such petty business. I am fully aware that you are assistant chief of the Lending Division of the Shinjuku branch of the Tokyo Security Trust Bank. But my visit has nothing to do with the repayment of loans. I have come here to save Tokyo from destruction."

Katagiri scanned the room for a hidden TV camera in case he was being made the butt of some huge, terrible joke. But there was no camera. It was a small apartment. There was no place for anyone to hide.

"No," Frog said, "we are the only ones here. I know you are thinking that I must be mad, or that you are having some kind of dream, but I am not crazy and you are not dreaming. This is absolutely, positively serious."

"To tell you the truth, Mr. Frog—"

"Please," Frog said, raising one finger again. "Call me 'Frog.'"

"To tell you the truth, Frog," Katagiri said, "I can't quite understand what is going on here. It's not that I don't trust you, but I don't seem to be able to grasp the situation exactly. Do you mind if I ask you a question or two?"

"Not at all, not at all," Frog said. "Mutual understanding is of critical importance. There are those who say that 'understanding' is merely the sum total of our misunderstandings, and while I do find this view interesting in its own way, I am afraid that we have no time to spare on pleasant digressions. The best thing would be for us to achieve mutual understanding via the shortest possible route. Therefore, by all means, ask as many questions as you wish."

"Now, you *are* a real frog, am I right?"

"Yes, of course, as you can see. A real frog is exactly what I am. A product neither of metaphor nor allusion nor deconstruction nor sampling nor any other such complex process, I am a genuine frog. Shall I croak for you?"

Frog tilted back his head and flexed the muscles of his huge throat. *Ribit! Ri-i-i-bit! Ribit-ribit-ribit! Ribit! Ribit! Ri-i-i-bit!* His gigantic croaks rattled the pictures hanging on the walls.

"Fine, I see, I see!" Katagiri said, worried about the thin walls of the cheap apartment house in which he lived. "That's great. You are, without question, a real frog."

"One might also say that I am the sum total of all frogs. Nonetheless, this does nothing to change the fact that I am a frog. Anyone claiming that I am not a frog would be a dirty liar. I would smash such a person to bits!"

Katagiri nodded. Hoping to calm himself, he picked up his cup and swallowed a mouthful of tea. "You said before that you have come here to save Tokyo from destruction?"

"That is what I said."

"What kind of destruction?"

"Earthquake," Frog said with the utmost gravity.

Mouth dropping open, Katagiri looked at Frog. And Frog, saying nothing, looked at Katagiri. They went on staring at each other like this for some time. Next it was Frog's turn to open his mouth.

"A very, very big earthquake. It is set to strike Tokyo at eight-thirty a.m. on February 18. Three days from now. A much bigger earthquake than the one that struck Kobe last month. The number of dead from such a quake would probably exceed a hundred and fifty thousand—mostly from accidents involving the commuter system: derailments, falling vehicles, crashes, the collapse of elevated expressways and rail lines, the crushing of subways, the explosion of tanker trucks. Buildings will be transformed into piles of rubble, their inhabitants crushed to death. Fires everywhere, the road system in a state of collapse, ambulances and fire trucks useless, people just lying there, dying. A hundred and fifty thousand of them! Pure hell. People will be made to realize what a fragile condition the intensive collectivity known as 'city' really is." Frog said this with a gentle shake of the head. "The epicenter will be close to the Shinjuku ward office."

"Close to the Shinjuku ward office?"

"To be precise, it will hit directly beneath the Shinjuku branch of the Tokyo Security Trust Bank."

A heavy silence followed.

"And you," Katagiri said, "are planning to stop this earth-quake?"

"Exactly," Frog said, nodding. "That is exactly what I propose to do. You and I will go underground beneath the Shinjuku branch of the Tokyo Security Trust Bank to do mortal combat with Worm."

As a member of the Trust Bank Lending Division, Katagiri had fought his way through many a battle. He had weathered sixteen years of daily combat since the day he graduated from the university and joined the bank's staff. He was, in a word, a collection officer—a post that carried little popularity. Everyone in his division preferred to make loans, especially at the time of the bubble. They had so much money in those days that almost any likely piece of collateral—be it land or stock—was enough to convince loan officers to give away whatever they were asked for, the bigger the loan the better their reputations in the company. Some loans, though, never made it back to the bank: they got "stuck to the bottom of the pan." It was Katagiri's job to take care of those. And when the bubble burst, the work piled on. First stock prices fell, and then land values, and collateral lost all significance. "Get out there," his boss commanded him, "and squeeze whatever you can out of them."

The Kabukicho neighborhood of Shinjuku was a labyrinth of violence: old-time gangsters, Korean mobsters, Chinese mafia, guns and drugs, money flowing beneath the surface from one murky den to another, people vanishing every now and then like a puff of smoke. Plunging into Kabukicho to collect a bad debt, Katagiri had been surrounded more than once by mobsters threatening to kill him, but he had never been frightened. What good would it have done them to kill one man running around for the bank? They could stab him if they wanted to. They could beat him up. He was perfect for the job: no wife, no kids, both parents dead, brother and sister he had put through college married off. So what if they killed him? It wouldn't change anything for anybody—least of all for Katagiri himself.

It was not Katagiri but the thugs surrounding him who got nervous when they saw him so calm and cool. He soon earned a kind of reputation in their world as a tough guy. Now, though, the tough Katagiri was at a total loss. What the hell was this frog talking about? Worm?

"Who is Worm?" he asked with some hesitation.

"Worm lives underground. He is a gigantic worm. When he gets angry, he causes earthquakes," Frog said. "And right now he is very, very angry."

"What is he angry *about*?" Katagiri asked.

"I have no idea," Frog said. "Nobody knows what Worm is thinking inside that murky head of his. Few have ever seen him. He is usually asleep. That's what he really likes to do: take long, long naps. He goes on sleeping for years—decades—in the warmth and darkness underground. His eyes, as you might imagine, have atrophied, his brain has turned to jelly as he sleeps. If you ask me, I'd guess he probably isn't thinking anything at all, just lying there and feeling every little rumble and reverberation that comes his way, absorbing them into his body, and storing them up. And then, through some kind of chemical process, he replaces most of them with rage. Why this happens I have no idea. I could never explain it."

Frog fell silent, watching Katagiri and waiting until his words had sunk in. Then he went on:

"Please don't misunderstand me, though. I feel no personal animosity toward Worm. I don't see him as the embodiment of evil. Not that I would want to be his friend, either: I just think that, as far as the world is concerned, it is in a sense *all right* for a being like him to exist. The world is like a great big overcoat, and it needs pockets of various shapes and sizes. But right at the moment Worm has reached the point where he is too dangerous to ignore. With all the different kinds of hatred he has absorbed and stored inside himself over the years, his heart and body have swollen to gargantuan proportions—bigger than ever before. And to make matters worse, last month's Kobe earthquake shook him out of the deep sleep he was enjoying. He experienced a revelation inspired by his profound rage: it was time now for him, too, to cause a massive earthquake, and he'd do it here, in Tokyo. I know what I'm talking about, Mr. Katagiri: I have received reliable information on the timing and scale of the earthquake from some of my best bug friends."

Frog snapped his mouth shut and closed his round eyes in apparent fatigue.

"So what you're saying is," Katagiri said, "that you and I have to go underground together and fight Worm to stop the earthquake."

"Exactly."

Katagiri reached for his cup of tea, picked it up, and put it back. "I still don't get it," he said. "Why did you choose *me* to go with you?"

Frog looked straight into Katagiri's eyes and said, "I have always had the profoundest respect for you, Mr. Katagiri. For sixteen long years, you have silently accepted the most danger-ous, least glamorous assignments—the jobs that others have avoided—and you have carried them off beautifully. I know full well how difficult this has been for you, and I believe that neither your superiors nor your colleagues properly appreciate your ac-complishments. They are blind, the whole lot of them. But you, unappreciated and unpromoted, have never once complained.

"Nor is it simply a matter of your work. After your par-ents died, you raised your teenage brother and sister single-handedly, put them through college, and even arranged for them to marry, all at great sacrifice of your time and income, and at the expense of your own marriage prospects. In spite of this, your brother and sister have never once expressed grati-tude for your efforts on their behalf. Far from it: they have shown you no respect and acted with the most callous disre-gard for your loving-kindness. In my opinion, their behavior is unconscionable. I almost wish I could beat them to a pulp on your behalf. But you, meanwhile, show no trace of anger.

"To be quite honest, Mr. Katagiri, you are nothing much to look at, and you are far from eloquent, so you tend to be looked down upon by those around you. *I*, however, can see what a sensible and courageous man you are. In all of Tokyo, with its teeming millions, there is no one else I could trust as much as you to fight by my side."

"Tell me, Mr. Frog—" Katagiri said.

"Please," Frog said, raising one finger again. "Call me 'Frog.'"

"Tell me, Frog," Katagiri said, "how do you know so much about me?"

"Well, Mr. Katagiri, I have not been frogging all these years for nothing. I keep my eye on the important things in life."

"But still, Frog," Katagiri said, "I'm not particularly strong, and I don't know anything about what's happening underground. I don't have the kind of muscle it will take to fight Worm in the darkness. I'm sure you can find somebody a lot stronger than me—a man who does karate, say, or a Self-Defense Force commando."

Frog rolled his large eyes. "To tell you the truth, Mr. Katagiri," he said, "*I'm* the one who will do all the fighting. But I can't do it alone. This is the key thing: I need your courage and your passion for justice. I need you to stand behind me and say, 'Way to go, Frog! You're doing great! I know you can win! You're fighting the good fight!'"

Frog opened his arms wide, then slapped his webbed hands down on his knees again.

"In all honesty, Mr. Katagiri, the thought of fighting Worm in the dark frightens me, too. For many years I lived as a pacifist, loving art, living with nature. Fighting is not something I like to do. I do it because I have to. And this particular fight will be a fierce one, that is certain. I may not return from it alive. I may lose a limb or two in the process. But I cannot—I *will* not—run away. As Nietzsche said, the highest wisdom is to have no fear. What I want from you, Mr. Katagiri, is for you to share your simple courage with me, to support me with your whole heart as a true friend. Do you understand what I am trying to tell you?"

None of this made any sense to Katagiri, but still he felt that—unreal as it sounded—he could believe whatever Frog said to him. Something about Frog—the look on his face, the way he spoke—had a simple honesty to it that appealed directly to the heart. After years of work in the toughest division of the Security Trust Bank, Katagiri possessed the ability to sense such things. It was all but second nature to him.

"I know this must be difficult for you, Mr. Katagiri. A huge frog comes barging into your place and asks you to believe all these outlandish things. Your reaction is perfectly natural. And so I intend to provide you with proof that I exist. Tell me, Mr. Katagiri, you have been having a great deal of trouble recovering a loan the bank made to Big Bear Trading, have you not?"

"That's true," Katagiri said.

"Well, they have a number of extortionists working behind the scenes, and those individuals are mixed up with the mobsters. They're scheming to make the company go bankrupt and get out of its debts. Your bank's loan officer shoved a pile of cash at them without a decent background check, and, as usual, the one who's left to clean up after him is you, Mr. Katagiri. But you're having a hard time sinking your teeth into these fellows: they're no pushovers. And there may be a powerful politician backing them up. They're into you for seven hundred million yen. That is the situation you are dealing with, am I right?"

"You certainly are."

Frog stretched his arms out wide, his big green webs opening like pale wings. "Don't worry, Mr. Katagiri. Leave everything to me. By tomorrow morning, old Frog will have your problems solved. Relax and have a good night's sleep."

With a big smile on his face, Frog stood up. Then, flattening himself like a dried squid, he slipped out through the gap at the side of the closed door, leaving Katagiri all alone. The two teacups on the kitchen table were the only indication that Frog had ever been in Katagiri's apartment.

The moment Katagiri arrived at work the next morning at nine, the phone on his desk rang.

"Mr. Katagiri," said a man's voice. It was cold and businesslike. "My name is Shiraoka. I am an attorney with the Big Bear case. I received a call from my client this morning with regard to the pending loan matter. He wants you to know that he will take full responsibility for returning the entire amount requested by the due date. He will also give you a signed memorandum to that effect. His only request is that you do not send Frog to his home again. I repeat: he wants you to ask Frog never to visit his home again. I myself am not entirely sure what this is supposed to mean, but I believe it should be clear to you, Mr. Katagiri. Am I correct?"

"You are indeed," Katagiri said.

"You will be kind enough to convey my message to Frog, I trust."

"That I will do. Your client will never see Frog again."

"Thank you very much. I will prepare the memorandum for you by tomorrow."

"I appreciate it," Katagiri said.

The connection was cut.

Frog visited Katagiri in his Trust Bank office at lunchtime. "That Big Bear case is working out well for you, I presume?"

Katagiri glanced around uneasily.

"Don't worry," Frog said. "You are the only one who can see me. But now I am sure you realize that I actually exist. I am not a product of your imagination. I can take action and produce results. I am a real, living being."

"Tell me, Mr. Frog—"

"Please," Frog said, raising one finger. "Call me 'Frog.'"

"Tell me, Frog," Katagiri said, "what did you do to them?"

"Oh, nothing much," Frog said. "Nothing much more complicated than boiling Brussels sprouts. I just gave them a little scare. A touch of psychological terror. As Joseph Conrad once wrote, true terror is the kind that men feel toward their imagination. But never mind that, Mr. Katagiri. Tell me about the Big Bear case. It's going well?"

Katagiri nodded and lit a cigarette. "Seems to be."

"So, then, have I succeeded in gaining your trust with regard to the matter I broached to you last night? Will you join me to fight against Worm?"

Sighing, Katagiri removed his glasses and wiped them. "To tell you the truth, I'm not too crazy about the idea, but I don't suppose that's enough to get me out of it."

"No," Frog said. "It is a matter of responsibility and honor. You may not be too 'crazy' about the idea, but we have no choice: you and I must go underground and face Worm. If we should happen to lose our lives in the process, we will gain no one's sympathy. And even if we manage to defeat Worm, no one will praise us. No one will ever know that such a battle even raged far beneath their feet. Only you and I will know, Mr. Katagiri. However it turns out, ours will be a lonely battle."

Katagiri looked at his own hand for a while, then watched the smoke rising from his cigarette. Finally, he spoke. "You know, Mr. Frog, I'm just an ordinary person."

"Make that 'Frog,' please," Frog said, but Katagiri let it go.

"I'm an absolutely ordinary guy. Less than ordinary. I'm going bald, I'm getting a potbelly, I turned forty last month. My feet are flat. The doctor told me recently that I have diabetic tendencies. It's been three months or more since I last slept with a woman—and I had to pay for it. I do get some recognition within the division for my ability to collect on loans, but no real respect. I don't have a single person who likes me, either at work or in my private life. I don't know how to talk to people, and I'm bad with strangers, so I never make friends. I have no athletic ability, I'm tone-deaf, short, phimotic, nearsighted—*and* astigmatic. I live a horrible life. All I do is eat, sleep, and shit. I don't know why I'm even living. Why should a person like me have to be the one to save Tokyo?"

"Because, Mr. Katagiri, Tokyo can *only* be saved by a person like you. And it's *for* people like you that I am trying to save Tokyo."

Katagiri sighed again, more deeply this time. "All right then, what do you want me to do?"

Frog told Katagiri his plan. They would go underground on the night of February 17 (one day before the earthquake was scheduled to happen). Their way in would be through the basement boiler room of the Shinjuku branch of the Tokyo Security Trust Bank. They would meet there late at night (Katagiri would stay in the building on the pretext of working overtime). Behind a section of wall was a vertical shaft, and they would find Worm at the bottom by climbing down a 150-foot rope ladder.

"Do you have a battle plan in mind?" Katagiri asked.

"Of course I do. We would have no hope of defeating an enemy like Worm without a battle plan. He is a slimy creature: you can't tell his mouth from his anus. And he's as big as a commuter train."

"What *is* your battle plan?"

After a thoughtful pause, Frog answered, "Hmm, what is it they say—'Silence is golden'?"

"You mean I shouldn't ask?"

"That's one way of putting it."

"What if I get scared at the last minute and run away? What would you do then, Mr. Frog?"

" 'Frog.' "

"Frog. What would you do then?"

Frog thought about this a while and answered, "I would fight on alone. My chances of beating him by myself are perhaps just slightly better than Anna Karenina's chances of beating that speeding locomotive. Have you read *Anna Karenina*, Mr. Katagiri?"

When he heard that Katagiri had not read the novel, Frog gave him a look as if to say, What a shame. Apparently Frog was very fond of *Anna Karenina*.

"Still, Mr. Katagiri, I do not believe that you will leave me to fight alone. I can tell. It's a question of balls—which, unfortunately, I do not happen to possess. Ha ha ha ha!" Frog laughed with his mouth wide open. Balls were not all that Frog lacked. He had no teeth, either.

Unexpected things do happen, however.

Katagiri was shot on the evening of February 17. He had finished his rounds for the day and was walking down the street in Shinjuku on his way back to the Trust Bank when a young man in a leather jacket leaped in front of him. The man's face was a blank, and he gripped a small black gun in one hand. The gun was *so* small and *so* black it hardly looked real. Katagiri stared at the object in the man's hand, not registering the fact that it was aimed at him and that the man was pulling the trigger. It all happened too quickly: it didn't make sense to him. But the gun in fact went off.

Katagiri saw the barrel jerk in the air and, at the same moment, felt an impact as though someone had struck his right shoulder with a sledgehammer. He felt no pain, but the blow sent him sprawling on the sidewalk. The leather briefcase in his right hand went flying in the other direction. The man aimed the gun at him again. A second shot rang out. A small eatery's sidewalk signboard exploded before his eyes. He heard people screaming. His eyeglasses had flown off, and everything was a blur. He was vaguely aware that the man was approaching with the pistol pointed at him. I'm going to die, he thought. Frog had said that true terror is the kind that men feel toward their imagination. Katagiri cut the switch of his imagination and sank into a weightless silence.

———

When he woke up, he was in bed. He opened one eye, took a moment to survey his surroundings, and then opened the other eye. The first thing that entered his field of vision was a metal stand by the head of the bed and an intravenous feeding tube that stretched from the stand to where he lay. Next he saw a nurse dressed in white. He realized that he was lying on his back on a hard bed and wearing some strange piece of clothing, under which he seemed to be naked.

Oh yeah, he thought, I was walking along the sidewalk when some guy shot me. Probably in the shoulder. The right one. He relived the scene in his mind. When he remembered the small black gun in the young man's hand, his heart made a disturbing thump. The sons of bitches were trying to kill me! he thought. But it looks as if I made it through OK. My memory is fine. I don't have any pain. And not just pain: I don't have any feeling at all. I can't lift my arm . . .

The hospital room had no windows. He could not tell whether it was day or night. He had been shot just before five in the evening. How much time had passed since then? Had the hour of his nighttime rendezvous with Frog gone by? Katagiri searched the room for a clock, but without his glasses he could see nothing at a distance.

"Excuse me," he called to the nurse.

"Oh, good, you're finally awake," the nurse said.

"What time is it?"

She looked at her watch.

"Nine-fifteen."

"P.M.?"

"Don't be silly, it's morning!"

"Nine-fifteen a.m.?" Katagiri groaned, barely managing to lift his head from the pillow. The ragged noise that emerged from his throat sounded like someone else's voice. "Nine-fifteen a.m. on February 18?"

"Right," the nurse said, lifting her arm once more to check the date on her digital watch. "Today is February 18, 1995."

"Wasn't there a big earthquake in Tokyo this morning?"

"In Tokyo?"

"In Tokyo."

The nurse shook her head. "Not as far as I know."

He breathed a sigh of relief. Whatever had happened, the earthquake at least had been averted.

"How's my wound doing?"

"Your wound?" she asked. "What wound?"

"Where I was shot."

"Shot?"

"Yeah, near the entrance to the Trust Bank. Some young guy shot me. In the right shoulder, I think."

The nurse flashed a nervous smile in his direction. "I'm sorry, Mr. Katagiri, but you haven't been shot."

"I haven't? Are you sure?"

"As sure as I am that there was no earthquake this morning."

Katagiri was stunned. "Then what the hell am I doing in a hospital?"

"Somebody found you lying in the street, unconscious. In the Kabukicho neighborhood of Shinjuku. You didn't have any external wounds. You were just out cold. And we still haven't found out why. The doctor's going to be here soon. You'd better talk to him."

Lying in the street unconscious? Katagiri was sure he had seen the pistol go off aimed at him. He took a deep breath and tried to get his head straight. He would start by putting all the facts in order.

"What you're telling me is, I've been lying in this hospital bed, unconscious, since early evening yesterday, is that right?"

"Right," the nurse said. "And you had a really bad night, Mr. Katagiri. You must have had some awful nightmares. I heard you yelling, 'Frog! Hey, Frog!' You did it a lot. You have a friend nicknamed 'Frog'?"

Katagiri closed his eyes and listened to the slow, rhythmic beating of his heart as it ticked off the minutes of his life. How much of what he remembered had actually happened, and how much was hallucination? Did Frog really exist, and had Frog fought with Worm to put a stop to the earthquake? Or had that just been part of a long dream? Katagiri had no idea what was true anymore.

Frog came to his hospital room that night. Katagiri awoke to find him in the dim light, sitting on a steel folding chair, his back against the wall. Frog's big, bulging green eyelids were closed in a straight slit.

"Frog!" Katagiri called out to him.

Frog slowly opened his eyes. His big white stomach swelled and shrank with his breathing.

"I meant to meet you in the boiler room at night the way I promised," Katagiri said, "but I had an accident in the evening—something totally unexpected—and they brought me here."

Frog gave his head a slight shake. "I know. It's OK. Don't worry. You were a great help to me in my fight, Mr. Katagiri."

"I was?"

"Yes, you were. You did a great job in your dreams. That's what made it possible for me to fight Worm to the finish. I have you to thank for my victory."

"I don't get it," Katagiri said. "I was unconscious the whole time. They were feeding me intravenously. I don't remember doing anything in my dreams."

"That's fine, Mr. Katagiri. It's better that you don't remember. The whole terrible fight occurred in the area of imagination. That is the precise location of our battlefield. It is there that we experience our victories and our defeats. Each and every one of us is a being of limited duration: all of us eventually go down to defeat. But as Ernest Hemingway saw so clearly, the ultimate value of our lives is decided not by how we win but by how we lose. You and I together, Mr. Katagiri, were able to prevent the annihilation of Tokyo. We saved a hundred and fifty thousand people from the jaws of death. No one realizes it, but that is what we accomplished."

"How did you manage to defeat Worm? And what did I do?"

"We gave everything we had in a fight to the bitter end. We—" Frog snapped his mouth shut and took one great breath, "—we used every weapon we could get our hands on, Mr. Katagiri. We used all the courage we could muster. Darkness was our enemy's ally. You brought in a foot-powered generator and used every ounce of your strength to fill the place with light. Worm tried to frighten you away with phantoms of the darkness, but you stood your ground. Darkness vied with light in a horrific battle, and in the light I grappled with the monstrous Worm. He coiled himself around me, and bathed me in his horrid slime. I tore him to shreds, but still he refused to die. All he did was divide into smaller pieces. And then—"

Frog fell silent, but soon, as if dredging up his last ounce of strength, he began to speak again. "Fyodor Dostoevsky, with unparalleled tenderness, depicted those who have been forsaken by God. He discovered the precious quality of human existence in the ghastly paradox whereby men who had invented God were forsaken by that very God. Fighting with Worm in the darkness, I found myself thinking of Dostoevsky's 'White Nights.' I . . ." Frog's words seemed to founder. "Mr. Katagiri, do you mind if I take a brief nap? I am utterly exhausted."

"Please," Katagiri said. "Take a good, deep sleep."

"I was finally unable to defeat Worm," Frog said, closing his eyes. "I did manage to stop the earthquake, but I was only able to carry our battle to a draw. I inflicted injury on him, and he on me. But to tell you the truth, Mr. Katagiri . . ."

"What is it, Frog?"

"I am, indeed, pure Frog, but at the same time I am a thing that stands for a world of un-Frog."

"Hmm, I don't get that at all."

"Neither do I," Frog said, his eyes still closed. "It's just a feeling I have. What you see with your eyes is not necessarily real. My enemy is, among other things, the me inside me.

Inside me is the un-me. My brain is growing muddy. The loco-motive is coming. But I really want you to understand what I'm saying, Mr. Katagiri."

"You're tired, Frog. Go to sleep. You'll get better."

"I am slowly, slowly returning to the mud, Mr. Katagiri. And yet . . . I . . ."

Frog lost his grasp on words and slipped into a coma. His arms hung down almost to the floor, and his big wide mouth drooped open. Straining to focus his eyes, Katagiri was able to make out deep cuts covering Frog's entire body. Discolored streaks ran through his skin, and there was a sunken spot on his head where the flesh had been torn away.

Katagiri stared long and hard at Frog, who sat there now wrapped in the thick cloak of sleep. As soon as I get out of this hospital, he thought, I'll buy *Anna Karenina* and "White Nights" and read them both. Then I'll have a nice long literary discus-sion about them with Frog.

Before long, Frog began to twitch all over. Katagiri assumed at first that these were just normal involuntary movements in sleep, but he soon realized his mistake. There was something unnatural about the way Frog's body went on jerking, like a big doll being shaken by someone from behind. Katagiri held his breath and watched. He wanted to run over to Frog, but his own body remained paralyzed.

After a while, a big lump formed over Frog's right eye. The same kind of huge, ugly boil broke out on Frog's shoulder and side, and then over his whole body. Katagiri could not imagine what was happening to Frog. He stared at the spectacle, barely breathing.

Then, all of a sudden, one of the boils burst with a loud pop. The skin flew off, and a sticky liquid oozed out, sending a horrible smell across the room. The rest of the boils started popping, one after another, twenty or thirty in all, flinging skin and fluid onto the walls. The sickening, unbearable smell filled the hospital room. Big black holes were left on Frog's body where the boils had burst, and wriggling, maggotlike worms of all shapes and sizes came crawling out. Puffy white maggots. After them emerged some kind of small centipedelike creatures, whose hundreds of legs made a creepy rustling sound. An endless stream of these things came crawling out of the holes. Frog's body—or the thing that must once have been Frog's body—was totally covered with these creatures of the night. His two big eyeballs fell from their sockets onto the floor, where they were devoured by black bugs with strong jaws. Crowds of slimy worms raced each other up the walls to the ceiling, where they covered the fluorescent lights and burrowed into the smoke alarm.

The floor, too, was covered with worms and bugs. They climbed up the lamp and blocked the light and, of course, they crept onto Katagiri's bed. Hundreds of them came burrowing under the covers. They crawled up his legs, under his bedgown, between his thighs. The smallest worms and maggots crawled inside his anus and ears and nostrils. Centipedes pried his mouth open and crawled inside one after another. Filled with an intense despair, Katagiri screamed.

Someone snapped a switch and light filled the room.

"Mr. Katagiri!" called the nurse. Katagiri opened his eyes to the light. His body was soaked in sweat. The bugs were gone. All they had left behind in him was a horrible slimy sensation.

"Another bad dream, eh? Poor dear." With quick, efficient movements the nurse readied an injection and stabbed the needle into his arm.

He took a long, deep breath and let it out. His heart was expanding and contracting violently.

"What were you dreaming about?"

Katagiri was having trouble differentiating dream from reality. "What you see with your eyes is not necessarily real," he told himself aloud.

"That's so true," said the nurse with a smile. "Especially where dreams are concerned."

"Frog," he murmured.

"Did something happen to Frog?" she asked.

"He saved Tokyo from being destroyed by an earthquake. All by himself."

"That's nice," the nurse said, replacing his near-empty intravenous feeding bottle with a new one. "We don't need any more awful things happening in Tokyo. We have plenty already."

"But it cost him his life. He's gone. I think he went back to the mud. He'll never come here again."

Smiling, the nurse toweled the sweat from his forehead. "You were very fond of Frog, weren't you, Mr. Katagiri?"

"Locomotive," Katagiri mumbled. "More than anybody." Then he closed his eyes and sank into a restful, dreamless sleep.

honey pie

"So Masakichi got his paws full of honey—way more honey than he could eat by himself—and he put it in a bucket, and do-o-o-wn the mountain he went, all the way to the town to sell his honey. Masakichi was the all-time Number One honey bear."

"Do bears have buckets?" Sala asked.

"Masakichi just happened to have one," Junpei explained. "He found it lying in the road, and he figured it would come in handy sometime."

"And it did."

"It really did. So Masakichi the Bear went to town and found a spot for himself in the square. He put up a sign: *Deee-licious Honey. All Natural. One Cup ¥ 200.*"

"Can bears write?"

"No, of course not," Junpei said. "There was a nice old man with a pencil sitting next to him, and he asked *him* to write it."

"Can bears count money?"

"Absolutely. Masakichi lived with people when he was just a cub, and they taught him how to talk and count money and stuff. Anyway, he was a very talented bear."

"Oh, so he was a little different from ordinary bears."

"Well, yes, just a little. Masakichi was a kind of special bear. And so the other bears, who weren't so special, tended to shun him."

"Shun him?"

"Yeah, they'd go like, 'Hey, what's with this guy, acting so special?' and keep away from him. Especially Tonkichi the tough guy. He really hated Masakichi."

"Poor Masakichi!"

"Yeah, really. Meanwhile, Masakichi *looked* just like a bear, and so the people would say, 'OK, he knows how to count, and he can talk and all, but when you get right down to it he's still a bear.' So Masakichi didn't really belong to either world—the bear world or the people world."

"Poor, poor Masakichi! Didn't he have any friends?"

"Not one. Bears don't go to school, you know, so there's no place for them to make friends."

"*I* have friends," Sala said. "In preschool."

"Of course you do," Junpei said.

"Do *you* have friends, Jun?" "Uncle Junpei" was too long for her, so Sala just called him "Jun."

"Your daddy is my absolute bestest friend from a long, long time ago. And so's your mommy."

"It's good to have friends."

"It *is* good," Junpei said. "You're right about that."

Junpei often made up stories for Sala when she went to bed.

And whenever she didn't understand something, she would ask him to explain. Junpei gave a lot of thought to his answers. Sala's questions were always sharp and interesting, and while he was thinking about them he could also come up with new twists to the story.

Sayoko brought a glass of warm milk.

"Junpei is telling me the story of Masakichi the bear," Sala said. "He's the all-time Number One honey bear, but he doesn't have any friends."

"Oh really? Is he a big bear?" Sayoko asked.

Sala gave Junpei an uneasy look. "Is Masakichi big?"

"Not so big," he said. "In fact, he's kind of on the small side. For a bear. He's just about *your* size, Sala. And he's a very sweet-tempered little guy. When he listens to music, he doesn't listen to rock or punk or that kind of stuff. He likes to listen to Schubert all by himself."

Sayoko hummed a little "Trout."

"He listens to music?" Sala asked. "Does he have a CD player or something?"

"He found a boom box lying on the ground one day. He picked it up and brought it home."

"How come all this stuff just happens to be lying around in the mountains?" Sala asked with a note of suspicion.

"Well, it's a very, very steep mountain, and the hikers get all faint and dizzy, and they throw away tons of stuff they don't need. Right there by the road, like, 'Oh man, this pack is so heavy, I feel like I'm gonna die! I don't need this bucket anymore. I don't need this boom box anymore.' Like that. So Masakichi finds everything he needs lying in the road."

"Mommy knows just how they feel," Sayoko said. "Sometimes you want to throw everything away."

"Not *me*," Sala said.

"That's 'cause you're such a greedy little thing," Sayoko said.

"I am *not* greedy," Sala protested.

"No," Junpei said, finding a gentler way to put it: "You're just young and full of energy, Sala. Now hurry and drink your milk so I can tell you the rest of the story."

"OK," she said, wrapping her little hands around the glass and drinking the warm milk with great care. Then she asked, "How come Masakichi doesn't make honey pies and sell them? I think the people in the town would like that better than just plain honey."

"An excellent point," Sayoko said with a smile. "Think of the profit margin!"

"Ah, yes, creating new markets through value added," Junpei said. "This girl will be a real entrepreneur someday."

It was almost two a.m. by the time Sala went back to bed. Junpei and Sayoko checked to make sure she was asleep, then shared a can of beer at the kitchen table. Sayoko wasn't much of a drinker, and Junpei had to drive home.

"Sorry for dragging you out in the middle of the night," she said, "but I didn't know what else to do. I'm totally exhausted, and you're the only one who can calm her down. There was no way I was going to call Takatsuki."

Junpei nodded, took a slug of beer, and ate one of the crackers on the plate between them.

"Don't worry about me," he said. "I'm awake till the sun

comes up, and the roads are empty this time of night. It's no big deal."

"You were working on a story?"

Junpei nodded.

"How's it going?"

"Like always. I write 'em. They print 'em. Nobody reads 'em."

"*I* read them. *All* of them."

"Thanks. You're a nice person," Junpei said. "But the short story is on the way out. Like the slide rule. Anyhow, let's talk about Sala. Has she done this before?"

Sayoko nodded.

"A lot?"

"Almost every night. Sometime after midnight she gets these hysterical fits and jumps out of bed. She can't stop shaking. And I can't get her to stop crying. I've tried everything."

"Any idea what's wrong?"

Sayoko drank what was left of her beer, and stared at the empty glass.

"I think she saw too many news reports on the earthquake. It was too much for a four-year-old. She wakes up at around the time of the quake. She says a man woke her up, somebody she doesn't know. The Earthquake Man. He tries to put her in a little box—way too little for anyone to fit into. She tells him she doesn't want to get inside, but he starts yanking on her arm—so hard her joints crack—and he tries to stuff her inside. That's when she screams and wakes up."

"The Earthquake Man?"

"He's tall and skinny and old. After she's had the dream, she goes around turning on every light in the house and looks for him: in the closets, in the shoe cabinet in the front hall, under the beds, in all the dresser drawers. I tell her it was just a dream, but she won't listen to me. And she won't go to bed until she's looked everywhere he could possibly hide. That takes at least two hours, by which time I'm wide awake. I'm so sleep-deprived I can hardly stand up, let alone work."

Sayoko almost never spilled out her feelings like this.

"Try not to watch the news," Junpei said. "Don't even turn on the TV. The earthquake's all they're showing these days."

"I almost never watch TV anymore. But it's too late now. The Earthquake Man just keeps coming. I went to the doctor, but all he did was give me some kind of sleeping pill to humor me."

Junpei thought for a while.

"How about we go to the zoo on Sunday? Sala says she wants to see a real bear."

Sayoko narrowed her eyes and looked at him. "Maybe. It just might change her mood. Let's do it—the four of us. It's been ages. You call Takatsuki, OK?"

Junpei was thirty-six, born and bred in the city of Nishi-nomiya, Hyogo Prefecture, a quiet residential area in the Shukugawa district. His father owned a pair of jewelry stores, one in Osaka, one in Kobe. He had a sister six years his junior. After a time at a private high school in Kobe, he entered Waseda University in Tokyo. He had passed the entrance exams in both the business and the literature departments. He chose the literature department without the slightest hesitation and told his parents that he had entered the business department. They would never have paid for him to study literature, and

Junpei had no intention of wasting four precious years studying the workings of the economy. All he wanted was to study
literature, and then to become a novelist.

At the university, he made two friends, Takatsuki and
Sayoko. Takatsuki came from the mountains of Nagano. Tall
and broad-shouldered, he had been the captain of his high-
school soccer team. It had taken him two years of studying to
pass the entrance exam, so he was a year older than Junpei.
Practical and decisive, he had the kind of looks that made
people take to him right away, and he naturally assumed a leader-
ship role in any group. But he had trouble reading books; he
had entered the literature department because its exam was the
only one he could pass. "What the hell," he said in his positive
way. "I'm going to be a newspaper reporter, so I'll let them
teach me how to write."

Junpei did not understand why Takatsuki had any interest in
befriending him. Junpei was the kind of person who liked to sit
alone in his room reading books or listening to music, and he
was terrible at sports. Awkward with strangers, he rarely made
friends. Still, for whatever reason, Takatsuki seemed to have
decided the first time he saw Junpei in class that he was going
to make him a friend. He tapped Junpei on the shoulder and
said, "Hey, let's get something to eat." And by the end of the
day they had opened their hearts to each other.

Takatsuki had Junpei with him when he adopted the same
approach with Sayoko. He tapped her on the shoulder and
said, "Hey, how about the three of us get something to eat?"
And so their tight little group was born. Junpei, Takatsuki, and
Sayoko did everything together. They shared lecture notes, ate

lunch in the campus dining hall, talked about their future over coffee between classes, took part-time jobs at the same place, went to all-night movies and rock concerts and walked all over Tokyo, and drank so much beer they even got sick together. In other words, they behaved like first-year college students the world over.

Sayoko was a real Tokyo girl. She came from the old part of town where the merchant class had lived for centuries, and her father ran a shop selling the exquisite little accessories that went with traditional Japanese dress. The business had been in the family for several generations, and it attracted an exclusive clientele that included several famous Kabuki actors. Sayoko had two elder brothers. The first had been groomed to inherit the shop, and the second worked in architectural design. She had graduated from an exclusive girls' prep school, entering the literature department of Waseda with plans to go on to graduate school in English Literature, and ultimately to an academic career. She read a lot, and she and Junpei were constantly exchanging novels and having intense conversations about them.

Sayoko had beautiful hair and intelligent eyes. She spoke quietly and with simple honesty, but deep down she had great strength. Her expressive mouth bore eloquent testimony to that. She was always casually dressed, without makeup, but she had a unique sense of humor, and her face would crinkle up mischievously whenever she made some funny remark. Junpei found that look of hers beautiful, and he knew that this was the girl he had been searching for. He had never fallen in love until he met Sayoko. He had attended a boys' high school and had had almost no opportunity to meet girls.

But Junpei could never bring himself to express his feelings to Sayoko. He knew that there would be no going back once the words left his mouth, and that she might take herself off somewhere far beyond his reach. At the very least, the perfectly balanced, comfortable relationship of Junpei, Takatsuki, and Sayoko would undergo a shift. So he told himself to leave things as they were for now and watch and wait.

In the end, Takatsuki was the first to make a move. "I hate to throw this at you all of a sudden," he told Junpei, "but I'm in love with Sayoko. I hope you don't mind."

This was midway through September. Takatsuki explained that he and Sayoko had become involved, almost by accident, while Junpei was home in Kansai for the summer vacation.

Junpei fixed his gaze on Takatsuki. It took him a few moments to understand what had happened, but when he did, it sank into him like a lead weight. He no longer had any choice in the matter. "No," he said, "I don't mind."

"I am *so* glad to hear that!" Takatsuki said with a huge grin. "You were the only one I was worried about. I mean, the three of us had such a great thing going, it was kind of like I beat you out. But anyway, Junpei, this had to happen sometime. You have to understand that. If not now, it was bound to happen sooner or later. The main thing is that I want the three of us to go on being friends. OK?"

For the next few days, Junpei felt as if he were trying to walk in deep sand. He skipped classes and work. He lay on the floor of his one-room apartment eating nothing but scraps from the refrigerator and slugging down whiskey whenever the impulse struck him. He thought seriously about quitting the university and going to some distant town where he knew no one and could spend the rest of his years doing manual labor. That would be the best lifestyle for him, he decided.

The fifth day after he stopped going to classes, Sayoko came to Junpei's apartment. She was wearing a navy blue sweatshirt and white cotton pants, and her hair was pinned back.

"Where have you been?" she asked. "Everybody's worried that you're dead in your room. Takatsuki asked me to check up on you. I guess he wasn't too keen on seeing the corpse himself. He's not as strong as he looks."

Junpei said he had been feeling sick.

"Yeah," she said, "you've lost weight, I think." She stared at him. "Want me to make you something to eat?"

Junpei shook his head. He didn't feel like eating, he said.

Sayoko opened the refrigerator and looked inside with a grimace. It contained only two cans of beer, a deceased cucumber, and some deodorizer. Sayoko sat down next to him. "I don't know how to put this, Junpei, but are you feeling bad about Takatsuki and me?"

Junpei said that he was not. And it was no lie. He was not feeling bad or angry. If, in fact, he was angry, it was at himself. For Takatsuki and Sayoko to become lovers was the most natural thing in the world. Takatsuki had all the qualifications. He himself had none. It was that simple.

"Go halves on a beer?" Sayoko asked.

"Sure."

She took a can of beer from the refrigerator and divided the contents between two glasses, handing one to Junpei. Then they drank in silence, separately.

"It's kind of embarrassing to put this into words," she said, "but I want to stay friends with you, Junpei. Not just for now, but even after we get older. A lot older. I love Takatsuki, but I need you, too, in a different way. Does that make me selfish?"

Junpei was not sure how to answer that, but he shook his head.

Sayoko said, "To understand something and to put that something into a form you can see with your own eyes are two completely different things. If you could manage to do both equally well, though, living would be a lot simpler."

Junpei stared at her in profile. He had no idea what she was trying to say. Why does my brain always have to work so slowly? he wondered. He looked up, and for a long time his half-focused eyes traced the shape of a stain on the ceiling. What would have happened if he had confessed his love to Sayoko before Takatsuki? To this Junpei could find no answer. All he knew for sure was that such a thing could never have happened. Ever.

He heard the sound of tears falling on the tatami, an oddly magnified sound. For a moment he wondered if he was crying without being aware of it. But then he realized that Sayoko was the one who was crying. She had hung her head between her knees, and now, though she made no sound, her shoulders were trembling.

Almost unconsciously, he reached out and put a hand on her shoulder. Then he drew her gently toward him. She did not resist. He wrapped his arms around her and pressed his lips to hers. She closed her eyes and let her lips come open. Junpei caught the scent of tears, and drew breath from her mouth. He felt the softness of her breasts against him. Inside his head, he felt some kind of huge switching of places. He even heard the sound it made, like the creaking of every joint in the world. But that was all. As if regaining consciousness, Sayoko moved her face back and down, pushing Junpei away.

"No," she said quietly, shaking her head. "We can't do this. It's wrong."

Junpei apologized. Sayoko said nothing. They remained that way, in silence, for a long time. The sound of a radio came in through the open window, riding on a breeze. It was a popular song. Junpei felt sure he would remember it till the day he died. In fact, though, try as he might after that, he was never able to bring back the title or the melody.

"You don't have to apologize," Sayoko said. "It's not your fault."

"I think I'm confused," he said honestly.

She reached out and laid her hand on his. "Come back to school, OK? Tomorrow? I've never had a friend like you before. You give me so much. I hope you realize that."

"So much, but not enough," he said.

"That's not true," she said with a resigned lowering of her head. "That is so not true."

Junpei went to his classes the next day, and the tight-knit three-some of Junpei, Takatsuki, and Sayoko continued through graduation. Junpei's short-lived desire to disappear disappeared itself with almost magical ease. When he held her in his arms that day in his apartment and pressed his lips to hers, something inside him settled down where it belonged. At least he no longer felt confused. The decision had been made, even if he had not been the one to make it.

Sayoko would sometimes introduce Junpei to old high-school classmates of hers, and they would double-date. He saw a lot of one of the girls, and it was with her that he had sex for the first time, just before his twentieth birthday. But his heart was always somewhere else. He was respectful, kind, and tender to her, but never really passionate or devoted. The only times Junpei became passionate and devoted were when he was alone, writing stories. His girlfriend eventually went elsewhere in search of true warmth. This pattern repeated itself any number of times.

When he graduated, Junpei's parents discovered he had been majoring in literature, not business, and things turned ugly. His father wanted him to come back to Kansai and take over the family firm, but Junpei had no intention of doing that. He wanted to stay in Tokyo and keep writing fiction. There was no room for compromise on either side, and a violent argument ensued. Words were spoken that should not have been. Junpei never saw his parents again, and he was convinced that it had to be that way. Unlike his sister, who always managed to compromise and get along with their parents, Junpei had done nothing but clash with them from the time he was a child. So, he thought with a bitter smile, he had finally been disowned: the upright Confucian parents renounce the decadent scribbler—it was like something out of the Twenties.

Junpei never applied for regular employment, but took a series of part-time jobs that helped him to scrape by as he continued to write. Whenever he finished a story, he showed it to Sayoko to get her honest opinion, then revised it according to her suggestions. Until she pronounced a piece good, he would rewrite again and again, carefully and patiently. He had no other mentor, and he belonged to no writers' group. The one faint lamp he had to guide him was Sayoko's advice.

When he was twenty-four, a story of his won the new writer's prize from a literary magazine, and it was also nominated for the Akutagawa Prize, the coveted gateway to a successful career in fiction. Over the next five years, he was nominated four times for the Akutagawa Prize, but he never won it. He remained the eternally promising candidate. A typical opinion from a judge on the prize committee would say: "For such a young author, this is writing of very high quality, with remarkable examples of both the creation of scene and psychological analysis. But the author has a tendency to let sentiment take over from time to time, and the work lacks both freshness and novelistic sweep."

Takatsuki would laugh when he read such things. "These guys are off their rockers. What the hell is 'novelistic sweep'? Real people don't use words like that. 'Today's sukiyaki was lacking in beefistic sweep.' Ever hear anybody say anything like that?"

Junpei published two volumes of short stories before he turned thirty: *Horse in the Rain* and *Grapes*. *Horse in the Rain* sold ten thousand copies, *Grapes* twelve thousand. These were not bad figures for a new writer's short story collections, according to his editor. The reviews were generally favorable, but none gave his work passionate support.

Most of Junpei's stories depicted the course of unrequited young love. Their conclusions were always dark, and somewhat sentimental. Everyone agreed they were well written, but they stood unmistakably apart from the more fashionable literature of the day. Junpei's style was lyrical, the plots rather old-fashioned. Readers of his generation were looking for a more inventive style and grittier storylines. This was the age of video games and rap music, after all. Junpei's editor urged him to try a novel. If he never wrote anything but short stories, he would just keep dealing with the same material over and over again, and his fictional world would waste away. Writing a novel could open up whole new worlds for a writer. As a practical matter, too, novels attracted far more attention than stories. If he intended to have a long career, he should recognize that writing only short stories would be a hard way to make a living.

But Junpei was a born short story writer. He would shut himself in his room, let everything else go to hell, and turn out a first draft in three days of concentrated effort. After four more days of polishing, he would give the manuscript to Sayoko and his editor to read, then do more polishing in response to their remarks. Basically, though, the battle was won or lost in that first week. That was when everything that mattered in the story came together. His personality was suited to this way of working: total concentration of effort over a few short days; total concentration of imagery and language. Junpei felt only exhaustion when he thought about writing a novel. How could he possibly maintain and control that mental concentration for months at a time? That kind of pacing eluded him.

He tried, though. He tried over and over again, ending always in defeat. And so he gave up. Like it or not, he was going to have to make his living as a short story writer. That was his style. No amount of effort was going to change his personality. You couldn't turn a great second baseman into a home-run hitter.

Junpei did not need much money to support his austere bachelor's lifestyle. Once he had made what he needed for a given period, he would stop accepting work. He had only one silent cat to feed. The girlfriends he found were always the undemanding type, but even so, they would eventually get on his nerves, and he would come up with some excuse for ending the relationship. Sometimes, maybe once a month, he would wake at an odd time in the night with a feeling close to panic. I'm never going anywhere, he would tell himself. I can struggle all I want, but I'm never going anywhere. Then, he would either force himself to go to his desk and write, or drink until he could no longer stay awake. Except for these times, he lived a quiet, untroubled life.

Takatsuki had landed the job he had always wanted—reporting for a top newspaper. Since he never studied, his grades at university were nothing to brag about, but the impression he made at interviews was overwhelmingly positive, and he had pretty much been hired on the spot. Sayoko had entered graduate school, as planned. Life was all smooth sailing for them. They married six months after graduation, the ceremony as cheerful and busy as Takatsuki himself. They honeymooned in France, and bought a two-room condo a short commute from downtown Tokyo. Junpei would come over for dinner a couple of times a week, and the newlyweds always welcomed him warmly. It was almost as if they were more comfortable with Junpei around than when they were alone.

Takatsuki enjoyed his work at the newspaper. They assigned him first to the city desk and kept him running around from one scene of tragedy to the next, in the course of which he saw many dead bodies. "I can see a corpse now and not feel a thing," he said. Bodies severed by trains, charred in fires, discolored with age, the bloated cadavers of the drowned, shotgun victims with brains splattered, dismembered corpses with heads and arms sawed off. "Whatever distinguishes one lump of flesh from another when we're alive, we're all the same once we're dead," he said. "Just used-up shells."

Takatsuki was sometimes too busy to make it home until morning. Then Sayoko would call Junpei. She knew he was often up all night.

"Are you working? Can you talk?"

"Sure," he would say. "I'm not doing anything special."

They would discuss the books they had read, or things that had come up in their daily lives. Then they would talk about the old days, when they were all still free and wild and spontaneous. Conversations like that would inevitably bring back memories of the time when Junpei had held Sayoko in his arms: the smooth touch of her lips, the smell of her tears, the softness of her breasts against him, the transparent early autumn sunlight streaming onto the tatami floor of his apartment—these were never far from his thoughts.

Just after she turned thirty, Sayoko became pregnant. She was a graduate assistant at the time, but she took a break from her job to have a baby. The three of them came up with names, but they settled in the end on Junpei's suggestion—"Sala." "I love the sound of it," Sayoko told him. There were no complications with the birth, and that night Junpei and Takatsuki found themselves together without Sayoko for the first time in a long while. Junpei had brought over a bottle of single malt to celebrate, and they emptied it together at the kitchen table.

"Why does time shoot by like this?" Takatsuki said with a depth of feeling that was rare for him. "It seems like only yesterday I was a freshman, and then I met you, and then Sayoko, and the next thing I know I'm a father. It's weird, like I'm watching a movie in fast-forward. But you wouldn't understand, Junpei. You're still living the same way you did in college. It's like you never stopped being a student, you lucky bastard."

"Not so lucky," Junpei said, but he knew how Takatsuki felt. Sayoko was a mother now. It was as big a shock for Junpei as it was for Takatsuki. The gears of life had moved ahead a notch with a loud *ker-chunk*, and Junpei knew that they would never turn back again. The one thing he was not yet sure of was how he ought to feel about it.

"I couldn't tell you this before," Takatsuki said, "but I'm sure Sayoko was more attracted to you than she was to me." He was pretty drunk, but there was a far more serious gleam in his eye than usual.

"That's crazy," Junpei said with a smile.

"Like hell it is. I know what I'm talking about. You know how to put pretty words on a page, but you don't know shit about a woman's feelings. A drowned corpse does better than you. You had no idea how she felt about you, but I figured, what the hell, I was in love with her, and I couldn't find anybody better, so I had to have her. I still think she's the greatest woman in the world. And I still think it was my right to have her."

"Nobody's saying it wasn't," Junpei said.

Takatsuki nodded. "But you *still* don't get it. Not really. 'Cause you're so damned *stupid.* That's OK, though. I don't care if you're stupid. You're not such a bad guy. I mean, look, you're the guy that gave my daughter her *name.*"

"Yeah, OK, OK," Junpei said, "but I still don't *get* it when it comes to anything important."

"Exactly. When it comes to anything halfway important, you just don't *get* it. It's amazing to me that you can put a piece of fiction together."

"Yeah, well, that's a whole different thing."

"Anyhow, now there's four of us," Takatsuki said with a kind of sigh. "I wonder, though. Four of us. Four. Can that number be right?"

2

Junpei learned just before Sala's second birthday that Takatsuki and Sayoko were on the verge of breaking up. Sayoko seemed somewhat apologetic when she divulged the news to him. Takatsuki had had a lover since the time of Sayoko's pregnancy, she said, and he hardly ever came home anymore. It was someone he knew from work.

Junpei could not grasp what he was hearing, no matter how many details Sayoko was able to give him. Why did Takatsuki have to find himself another woman? He had declared Sayoko to be the greatest woman in the world the night Sala was born, and those words had come from deep in his gut. Besides, he was crazy about Sala. Why, in spite of that, did he have to abandon his family?

"I mean, I'm over at your house all the time, eating dinner with you guys, right? But I never sensed a thing. You were happiness itself—the perfect family."

"It's true," Sayoko said with a gentle smile. "We weren't lying to you or putting on an act. But quite separately from that, he got himself a girlfriend, and we can never go back to what we had. So we decided to split up. Don't let it bother you too much. I'm sure things will work out better now, in a lot of different ways."

"In a lot of different ways," she had said. The world is full of incomprehensible words, thought Junpei.

Sayoko and Takatsuki were divorced some months later. They concluded agreements on several specific issues without the slightest hang-up: no recriminations, no disputed claims. Takatsuki went to live with his girlfriend; he came to visit Sala once a week, and they all agreed that Junpei would try to be present at those times. "It would make things easier for both of us," Sayoko told Junpei. Easier? Junpei felt as if he had grown much older all of a sudden, though he had just turned thirty-three.

Sala called Takatsuki "Papa" and Junpei "Jun." The four of them were an odd pseudo-family. Whenever they got together, Takatsuki would be his usual talkative self, and Sayoko's behavior was perfectly natural, as though nothing had happened. If anything, she seemed even more natural than before in Junpei's eyes. Sala had no idea her parents were divorced. Junpei played his assigned role perfectly without the slightest objection. The three joked around as always and talked about the old days.

The only thing that Junpei understood about all this was that it was something the three of them needed.

"Hey, Junpei, tell me," Takatsuki said one January night when the two of them were walking home, breath white in the chill air. "Do you have somebody you're planning to marry?"

"Not at the moment," Junpei said.

"No girlfriend?"

"Nope, guess not."

"Why don't you and Sayoko get together?"

Junpei squinted at Takatsuki as if at some too-bright object. "Why?" he asked.

"'Why'?! Whaddya mean 'why'? It's so obvious! If nothing else, you're the only man I'd want to be a father to Sala."

"Is that the only reason you think I ought to marry Sayoko?"

Takatsuki sighed and draped his thick arm around Junpei's shoulders.

"What's the matter? Don't you like the idea of marrying Sayoko? Or is it the thought of stepping in after me?"

"That's not the problem. I just wonder if you can make, like, some kind of deal. It's a question of *decency*."

"This is no deal," Takatsuki said. "And it's got nothing to do with decency. You love Sayoko, right? You love Sala, too, right? That's the most important thing. I know you've got your own special hang-ups. Fine. I grant you that. But to me, it looks like you're trying to pull off your shorts without taking off your pants."

Junpei said nothing, and Takatsuki fell into an unusually long silence. Shoulder to shoulder, they walked down the road to the station, heaving white breath into the night.

"In any case," Junpei said, "you're an absolute idiot."

"I have to give you credit," Takatsuki said. "You're right on the mark. I don't deny it. I'm ruining my own life. But I'm telling you, Junpei, I couldn't help it. There was no way I could put a stop to it. I don't know any better than you do why it had to happen. There's no way to justify it, either. It just happened. And if not here and now, something like it would have happened sooner or later."

Junpei felt he had heard this speech before. "Do you remember what you said to me the night Sala was born? That Sayoko was the greatest woman in the world, that you could never find anyone to take her place."

"And it's still true. Nothing has changed where that's concerned. But that very fact can sometimes make things go bad."

"I don't know what you mean by that," Junpei said.

"And you never will," Takatsuki said with a shake of the head. He always had the last word.

Two years went by. Sayoko never went back to teaching. Junpei got an editor friend of his to send her a piece to translate, and she carried the job off with a certain flair. She had a gift for languages, and she knew how to write. Her work was fast, careful, and efficient, and the editor was impressed enough to bring her a new piece the following month that involved substantial literary translation. The pay was not very good, but it added to what Takatsuki was sending and helped Sayoko and Sala to live comfortably.

They all went on meeting at least once a week, as they always had. Whenever urgent business kept Takatsuki away, Sayoko, Junpei, and Sala would eat together. The table was quiet without Takatsuki, and the conversation turned to oddly mundane matters. A stranger would have assumed that the three of them were just a typical family.

Junpei went on writing a steady stream of stories, bringing out his fourth collection, *Silent Moon*, when he turned thirty-five. It received one of the prizes reserved for established writers, and the title story was made into a movie. Junpei also produced a few volumes of music criticism, wrote a book on ornamental gardening, and translated a collection of John Updike's short stories. All were well received. He had developed his own personal style which enabled him to transform the most deeply reverberating sounds and the subtle gradations of light and color into concise, convincing prose. Securing his position as a writer little by little, he had developed a steady readership, and a fairly stable income.

He continued to think seriously about asking Sayoko to marry him. On more than one occasion, he kept himself awake all night thinking about it, and for a time he was unable to work. But still, he could not make up his mind. The more he thought about it, the more it seemed to him that his relationship with Sayoko had been consistently directed by others. His position was always passive. Takatsuki was the one who had picked the two of them out of his class and created the threesome. Then he had taken Sayoko, married her, fathered a child with her, and divorced her. And now Takatsuki was the one who was urging Junpei to marry her. Junpei loved Sayoko, of course. About that there was no question. And now was the perfect time for him to be united with her. She probably wouldn't turn him down. But Junpei couldn't help thinking that things were just a bit *too* perfect. What was there left for *him* to decide? And so he went on wondering. And not deciding. And then the earthquake struck.

Junpei was in Barcelona at the time, writing a story for an airline magazine. He returned to his hotel in the evening to find the TV news filled with images of whole city blocks of collapsed buildings and black clouds of smoke. It looked like the aftermath of an air raid. Because the announcer was speaking in Spanish, it took Junpei a while to realize what city he was looking at, but it had to be Kobe. Several familiar-looking sights caught his eye. The expressway through Ashiya had collapsed. "You're from Kobe, aren't you?" his photographer asked.

"You're damn right I am," Junpei said.

But Junpei did not try to call his parents. The rift was too deep, and had gone on too long for there to be any hope of reconciliation. He flew back to Tokyo and resumed his normal life. He never turned on the television, and hardly looked at a newspaper. Whenever anyone mentioned the earthquake, he would clam up. It was an echo from a past that he had buried long ago. He hadn't set foot on those streets since his graduation, but still, the sight of the destruction laid bare raw wounds hidden somewhere deep inside him. The lethal, gigantic catastrophe seemed to change certain aspects of his life—quietly, but from the ground up. Junpei felt an entirely new sense of isolation. I have no roots, he thought. I'm not connected to anything.

Early on the Sunday morning that they had all planned to take Sala to the zoo to see the bears, Takatsuki called to say that he had to fly to Okinawa. He had managed at last to pry the promise of an hour-long one-on-one interview out of the governor. "Sorry, but you'll have to go to the zoo without me. I don't suppose Mr. Bear will be too upset if I don't make it."

So Junpei and Sayoko took Sala to the Ueno Zoo. Junpei held Sala in his arms and showed her the bears. She pointed to the biggest, blackest bear and asked, "Is that one Masakichi?"

"No no, that's not Masakichi," Junpei said. "Masakichi is smaller than that, and he's smarter-looking, too. That's the tough guy, Tonkichi."

"Tonkichi!" Sala yelled again and again, but the bear paid no attention. Then she looked at Junpei and said, "Tell me a story about Tonkichi."

"That's a hard one," Junpei said. "There aren't that many interesting stories about Tonkichi. He's just an ordinary bear. He can't talk or count money like Masakichi."

"But I bet you can tell me *something* good about him. One thing."

"You're absolutely right," Junpei said. "There's at least one good thing to tell about even the most ordinary bear. Oh yeah, I almost forgot. Well, Tonchiki—"

"Ton*kichi*!" Sala corrected him with a touch of impatience.

"Ah yes, sorry. Well, Tonkichi had one thing he could do really well, and that was catching salmon. He'd go to the river and crouch down behind a boulder and—*snap!*—he would grab himself a salmon. You have to be really fast to do something like that. Tonkichi wasn't the brightest bear on the mountain, but he could catch more salmon than any of the other bears. More than he could ever hope to eat. But he couldn't go to town to sell his extra salmon, because he didn't know how to talk."

"That's easy," Sala said. "All he had to do was trade his extra salmon for Masakichi's extra honey."

"You're right," Junpei said. "And that's what Tonkichi decided to do. You and he had exactly the same idea. So Tonkichi and Masakichi started trading salmon for honey, and before long they got to know each other really well. Tonkichi realized that Masakichi was not such a stuck-up bear after all, and Masakichi realized that Tonkichi was not just a tough guy. Before they knew it, they were best friends. They talked about *everything*. They traded know-how. They told each other jokes. Tonkichi worked hard at catching salmon, and Masakichi worked hard at collecting honey. But then one day, like a bolt from the blue, the salmon disappeared from the river."

"A bolt from the blue?"

"Like a flash of lightning from a clear blue sky," Sayoko explained. "All of a sudden, without warning."

"All of a sudden the salmon disappeared?" Sala asked with a somber expression. "But why?"

"Well, all the salmon in the world got together and decided they weren't going to swim up that river anymore, because a bear named Tonkichi was there, and he was so good at catching salmon. Tonkichi never caught another salmon after that. The best he could do was catch an occasional skinny frog and eat it, but the worst-tasting thing you could ever want to eat is a skinny frog."

"Poor Tonkichi!" Sala said.

"And that's how Tonkichi ended up being sent to the zoo?" Sayoko asked.

"Well, that's a long, long story," Junpei said, clearing his throat. "But basically, yes, that's what happened."

"Didn't Masakichi help Tonkichi?" Sala asked.

"He tried, of course. They were best friends, after all. That's what friends are for. Masakichi shared his honey with Tonkichi—for free! But Tonkichi said, 'I can't let you do that. It'd be like taking advantage of you.' Masakichi said, 'You don't have to be such a stranger with me, Tonkichi. If I were in your position, you'd do the same thing for me, I'm sure. You would, wouldn't you?'"

"Sure he would," Sala said.

"But things didn't stay that way between them for long," Sayoko interjected.

"Things didn't stay that way between them for long," Junpei said. "Tonkichi told Masakichi, 'We're supposed to be friends. It's not right for one friend to do all the giving and the other to do all the taking: that's not real friendship. I'm leaving this mountain now, Masakichi, and I'll try my luck somewhere else. And if you and I meet up again somewhere, we can be best friends again.' So they shook hands and parted. But after Tonkichi got down from the mountain, he didn't know enough to be careful in the outside world, so a hunter caught him in a trap. That was the end of Tonkichi's freedom. They sent him to the zoo."

"Poor Tonkichi," Sala said.

"Couldn't you have come up with a better ending? Like, everybody lives happily ever after?" Sayoko asked Junpei later.

"I haven't thought of one yet."

The three of them had dinner together as usual in Sayoko's apartment. Humming the "Trout," Sayoko boiled a pot of spaghetti and defrosted some tomato sauce while Junpei made a salad of green beans and onions. They opened a bottle of red wine and poured Sala a glass of orange juice. When they had finished eating and cleaning up, Junpei read to Sala from another picture book, but when bedtime came, she resisted.

"Please, Mommy, do the bra trick," she begged.

Sayoko blushed. "Not *now*," she said. "We have a *guest*."

"No we don't," Sala said. "Junpei's not a guest."

"What's this all about?" Junpei asked.

"It's just a silly game," Sayoko said.

"Mommy takes her bra off under her clothes, puts it on the table, and puts it back on again. She has to keep one hand on the table. And we time her. She's great!"

"*Sala!*" Sayoko growled, shaking her head. "It's just a little game we play at home. It's not meant for anybody else."

"Sounds like fun to me," Junpei said.

"Please, Mommy, show Junpei. Just once. If you do it, I'll go to bed right away."

"Oh, what's the use," Sayoko muttered. She took off her digital watch and handed it to Sala. "Now, you're not going to give me any more trouble about going to bed, right? OK, get ready to time me when I count to three."

Sayoko was wearing a baggy black crewneck sweater. She put both hands on the table and counted, "One . . . two . . . *three!*" Like a turtle pulling into its shell, she slipped her right hand up inside her sleeve, and then there was a light back-scratching kind of movement. Out came the right hand again, and the left hand went up its sleeve. Sayoko turned her head just a bit, and the left hand came out holding a white bra—a small one with no wires. Without the slightest wasted motion, the hand and bra went back up the sleeve, and the hand came out again. Then the right hand pulled in, poked around at the back, and came out again. The end. Sayoko rested her right hand on her left on the table.

"Twenty-five seconds," Sala said. "That's great, Mommy, a new record! Your best time so far was thirty-six seconds."

Junpei applauded. "Wonderful! Like magic."

Sala clapped her hands, too. Sayoko stood up and announced, "All right, show time is over. To bed, young lady. You promised."

Sala kissed Junpei on the cheek and went to bed.

Sayoko stayed with her until her breathing was deep and steady, then rejoined Junpei on the sofa. "I have a confession to make," she said. "I cheated."

"Cheated?"

"I didn't put the bra back on. I just pretended. I slipped it out from under my sweater and dropped it on the floor."

Junpei laughed. "What a terrible mother!"

"I wanted to make a new record," she said, narrowing her eyes with a smile. He hadn't seen her smile in that simple, natural way for a long time. Time wobbled on its axis inside him, like curtains stirring in a breeze. He reached for Sayoko's shoulder, and her hand took his. They came together on the sofa in a powerful embrace. With complete naturalness, they wrapped their arms around each other and kissed. It was as if nothing had changed since the time they were nineteen. Sayoko's lips had the same sweet fragrance.

"We should have been like this to begin with," she whispered after they had moved from the sofa to her bed. "But you didn't get it. You just didn't get it. Not till the salmon disappeared from the river."

They took off their clothes and held each other gently. Their hands groped clumsily, as if they were having sex for the first time in their lives. They took their time, until they knew they were ready, and then at last he entered Sayoko and she drew him in.

None of this seemed real to Junpei. In the half-light, he felt as if he were crossing a deserted bridge that went on and on forever. He moved, and she moved with him. Again and again he wanted to come, but he held back, fearing that, once it happened, the dream would end and everything would vanish.

Then, behind him, he heard a slight creaking sound. The bedroom door was easing open. The light from the hallway took the shape of the door and fell on the rumpled bedclothes. Junpei raised himself and turned to see Sala standing against the light. Sayoko held her breath and moved her hips away, pulling him out. Gathering the sheets to her breast, she used one hand to straighten her hair.

Sala was not crying or screaming. Her right hand gripping the doorknob, she just stood there, looking at the two of them but seeing nothing, her eyes focused on emptiness.

Sayoko called her name.

"The man told me to come here," Sala said in a flat voice, like someone who has just been ripped out of a dream.

"The man?" Sayoko asked.

"The Earthquake Man. He came and woke me up. He told me to tell you. He said he has the box ready for everybody. He said he's waiting with the lid open. He said I should tell you that, and you'd understand."

Sala slept in Sayoko's bed that night. Junpei stretched out on the living room sofa with a blanket, but he could not sleep. The TV faced the sofa, and for a very long time he stared at the dead screen. *They* were inside there. They were waiting with the box open. He felt a chill run up his spine, and no matter how long he waited, it would not go away.

He gave up trying to sleep and went to the kitchen. He made himself some coffee and sat at the table to drink it, but he felt something bunched up under one foot. It was Sayoko's bra. He picked it up and hung it on the back of a chair. It was a simple, lifeless piece of white underwear, not particularly big. It hung over the kitchen chair in the predawn darkness like some anonymous witness who had wandered in from a time long past.

He thought about his early days in college. He could still hear Takatsuki the first time they met in class saying, "Hey, let's get something to eat," in that warm way of his, and he could see Takatsuki's friendly smile that seemed to say, *Hey, relax. The world is just going to keep getting better and better.* Where did we eat that time? Junpei wondered, and what did we have? He couldn't remember, though he was sure it was nothing special.

"Why did you choose me to go to lunch with?" Junpei had asked him that day. Takatsuki smiled and tapped his temple with complete confidence. "I have a talent for picking the right friends at the right times in the right place."

He was right, Junpei thought, setting his coffee mug on the kitchen table. Takatsuki *did* have an intuitive knack for picking the right friends. But that was not enough. Finding one person to love over the long haul of one's life was quite a different matter from finding friends. Junpei closed his eyes and thought about the long stretch of time that had passed through him. He did not want to think of it as something he had merely used up without any meaning.

As soon as Sayoko woke in the morning, he would ask her to marry him. He was sure now. He couldn't waste another minute. Taking care not to make a sound, he opened the bedroom door and looked at Sayoko and Sala sleeping bundled in a comforter. Sala lay with her back to Sayoko, whose arm was draped on Sala's shoulder. He touched Sayoko's hair where it fell across the pillow, and caressed Sala's small pink cheek with the tip of his finger. Neither of them stirred. He eased himself down to the carpeted floor by the bed, his back against the wall, to watch over them in their sleep.

Eyes fixed on the hands of the wall clock, Junpei thought about the rest of the story for Sala—the tale of Masakichi and Tonkichi. He had to find a way out. He couldn't just leave Tonkichi stranded in the zoo. He had to save him. He retraced the story from the beginning. Before long, the vague outline of an idea began to sprout in his head, and, little by little, it took shape.

Tonkichi had the same thought as Sala: he would use the honey that Masakichi had collected to bake honey pies. It didn't take him long to realize that he had a real talent for making crisp, delicious honey pies. Masakichi took the honey pies to town and sold them to the people there. The people loved Tonkichi's pies and bought them by the dozen. So Tonkichi and Masakichi never had to separate again: they lived happily ever after in the mountains, best friends forever.

Sala would be sure to love the new ending. And so would Sayoko.

I want to write stories that are different from the ones I've written so far, Junpei thought: I want to write about people who dream and wait for the night to end, who long for the light so they can hold the ones they love. But right now I have to stay here and keep watch over this woman and this girl. I will never let anyone—not anyone—try to put them into that crazy box—not even if the sky should fall or the earth crack open with a roar.